Praise for Theolyn Boe...   ...sha *Chronicles*
Book One: Daughters of Terra:

"Ms. Boese has written a story that will bring out every emotion. This book leaves you wanting more of this fascinating series."

—Sherry, *Coffee Time Romance*

"Holy hotness, Batman. I think I combusted while reading Theolyn Boese's debut novel. The first book of the *Ta'e'sha Chronicles* series, *Daughters of Terra* knocked my socks off..."

—Francesca Haynes, *Just Erotic Romance Reviews*

Book Two: Shards of the Mind

"I loved Theolyn Boese's first book in this series and was more than pleased with its sequel. I am anxiously awaiting the next installment in this fantastic series. Theolyn knows how to create the perfect blend of elements to keep the readers enthralled."

—*Literary Nymphs Reviews*

"As a follow up to *Daughters of Terra*, *Shards of the Mind* is superb... The only problem I have is the wait for the next book in the series!"

Jambrea, *Joyfully Reviewed*

LooseId ®

ISBN 10: 1-59632-752-9
ISBN 13: 978-1-59632-752-8
SHARDS OF THE MIND: Book Two of The Ta'e'sha Chronicles
Copyright © July 2008 by Theolyn Boese
Originally released in e-book format in March 2008

Cover Illustration by Anne Cain
Cover Design by April Martinez

DISCLAIMER: Many of the acts described in our BDSM/fetish titles can be dangerous. Please do not try any new sexual practice, whether it be fire, rope, or whip play, without the guidance of an experienced practitioner. Neither Loose Id nor its authors will be responsible for any loss, harm, injury or death resulting from use of the information contained in any of its titles.

Printed in the U.S.A. by
Lightning Source, Inc.
1246 Heil Quaker Blvd
La Vergne TN 37086
www.lightningsource.com

SHARDS OF THE MIND

The Ta'e'sha Chronicles, Book Two

Theolyn Boese

Dedication

This one is for Mom and Dad, who love me even when they don't understand me, and for Tony because he does understand me, even when he wishes he didn't. That's where the gray (sorry, silver) hair came from. They've all had to put up with soggy shoulders, vetting boyfriends, and eating some of my more bizarre cooking failures. I love you guys.

Prologue

Tabet sneered at her brother and bared her teeth. "You do not have a larger following than I! We are equally worshipped!"

Teirnan snickered. "Oh yes, I do. They only worship you because you're the only female Goddess available to them. I doubt they even like you."

Tabet growled and looked down at the priests performing rites in her brother's temple. She flicked a finger; the High Priest's head exploded in a shower of blood and brain matter. The congregation began screaming as his headless body fell forward and landed on the goat they were preparing to sacrifice.

The goat immediately panicked and danced sideways, bleating in terror. It bucked and kicked, pulling the rope from the hand of the young priest holding it and bolting from the temple.

Her brother's followers stampeded after the terrified animal.

She smirked at him smugly.

He growled.

He looked down, grabbed air, and squeezed. A young priestess from his sister's temple screamed in agony as her bones were crushed to powder and her internal organs burst. She twitched briefly, blood trickling from her ears and eyes.

He flicked her body across the temple's altar. Chaos erupted among the remaining priestesses.

Tabet screamed with rage and slammed her fist down. The ground under his temple began to shake and part; the building sank from sight into the gaping hole that opened under it in a cloud of dust.

Teirnan glared at her and swirled a finger. Several people floated screaming into the air. He shook his hand sharply and the people flew in all directions, landing in broken, bleeding heaps.

"How dare you, you wretch!" she snarled, almost spitting.

"How dare I? How dare you touch my people?" he shouted angrily.

"They are not your people!"

"They are too!"

"Are not!"

"Are too!"

They glared at each other, panting.

Not taking her eyes from his she flicked her finger again. A huge stone statue of Teirnan fell in the courtyard. It landed in the center of a building, causing the two on either side to fall as well.

His eyes narrowed. He swept his hand across and up. Below, on the island they ruled, a huge wave suddenly swept over the land, destroying a city built in Tabet's honor.

They were both heedless to the screams of the injured and dying people they were supposed to protect and care for. They ignored the prayers for mercy, completely focused on fighting amongst themselves. The volcano in the center of the island erupted in protest of the abuse the land was being subjected to. Lava flowed, hot and slow, as ash spewed, clouding the air.

The carnage escalated, while they ignored everything around them, completely engrossed in what the other was doing.

"Enough!"

The twins jumped apart as a sexless voice boomed and rolled across the heavens, making their ears ring.

A swirling cloud of glowing color floated down between the two of them.

The God and Goddess of Atlantis stood frozen in place by the presence of the Great One.

The glowing shape drifted over the island, surveying the damage. Behind Tabet and Teirnan the other Gods and Goddesses of Earth began to appear. They looked around in confusion. Loud gasps of shock filled the heavens.

Below them the land was torn. Great wounds in the earth bled red mud where earthquakes had ripped the surface. People shook and stared sightlessly, holding the broken and maimed bodies of dead loved ones. Seawater sluggishly rolled back into the ocean, leaving the bodies of fish and a few of the Merfolk who had been heading to the island to trade goods. Several trees held the impaled bodies of more victims of the God and Goddess.

Horrified silence filled the area.

The Great One floated back to the two who had started this.

They hung their heads under the weight of the Great One's regard.

Several moments passed in heavy silence.

Finally, the Great One spoke. "Never have I seen such a blatant abuse of power." The Great One drifted around the other Gods and Goddesses assembled. "Look well, My children."

Heavy clouds began to form over the island. Snow slowly drifted from them and time froze. The snow thickened until they could no longer see the island.

"Tabet and Teirnan, you have shown yourselves unworthy of your Godhood. I take back the power I granted you upon your birth." The sexless voice buzzed angrily in the ears of all listening. "You have failed your children; you have failed your siblings." A beam of light grazed over the watching Gods and Goddesses. "And you have failed Me."

Tabet and Teirnan fell to their knees, gasping, as their power was stripped ruthlessly from them.

The Great One continued, "You shall take back all the pain you gave, and then you shall be purified in ice flame until I take you back within Me."

They both screamed as blue flame coated their bodies.

"I take your lands and people for My own until such a time as one is born who cares enough to free them and give them the lives they were meant to live."

The twins screamed as they writhed inside the shells of fire that burned, but did not consume. They did not have breath to beg for mercy, for the flames began to suck the air from their lungs and consume it, leaving them unable to speak or scream.

Those surrounding them watched in horror. The burning continued for several hours, until at last all the pain they had caused was given back to them and then the flames died away. Two white bodies were curled upon the ground. A breeze rose and the bodies crumbled into a fine ash that drifted away to mix with the snow still falling on Atlantis.

The Great One's voice echoed quietly to the watchers. "Remember, My children. Always remember. You are caretakers of your children and their lands. And I am the caretaker of you all. Should a poison seed begin to grow I will cull it out, lest it blight the others." The Great One drifted over the land again. "I take this land. Do not return here again unless I expressly permit it. Tell your children. Atlantis is no more."

With that, the Great One dissipated in a sparkling cloud.

The remaining Gods and Goddesses of Earth slowly left after a long look. They would remember this always. And fear it.

Chapter One

She screamed silently in her head as the fists came at her again and again. Pain bloomed along her body like great red flowers. It was never going to end. No one could stop him... Because they had no idea she was missing or that he had her...

Her stomach cramped again and more fluid gushed from between her legs. Her baby was dying. Or dead. It was too late.

The knife came out and flashed in the light, arching toward her face. He was going to cut out her eyes!

Thea woke with a gasp and sat up, slapping at the knife she could still see coming toward her. She panted as she became aware it had been another dream. They haunted her every time she closed her eyes.

She lay down again and curled up on her side. *It seems like I'm always tired now. And if I do sleep, it's only for a few minutes. I wonder how long the guys will put up with my tossing and turning before they send me to another room.* They had been very patient so far, but the interrupted sleep was starting to show on their faces as well as on hers.

She snuggled into the silky sheets covering their bed and shivered.

Several months ago she had awakened to find herself on this very bed and had been told she had been married to two men while she was unconscious and that the reason she had been taken was to give birth to their children. It had been a shock to say the least. However, after several weeks of living with them, she had settled into a routine and began making a place for herself. She had begun to accept, and even care for, the men as well.

A smile crossed her face as she thought about her two husbands. Kyrin, so stern and strong, with his muscular build and imposing nature. His golden skin and amber-brown hair made him look almost human. One had to look for the subtle differences that marked the Ta'e'shian people; their larger almond-shaped eyes and delicately pointed faces. He took his duties as ship's captain very seriously and was constantly updating himself on every little detail. He was firm and fair, and his crew loved him, even though they were careful to maintain a distance. She and Daeshen were the only ones who really got to see his softer side.

Daeshen. With his pale topaz blue hair, milky pale skin, and sweet smiles. He was soft-spoken and elegant, and he drew people to him with his friendly nature. She sometimes wondered if his brain ever stopped working, though. He always seemed to be thinking about something and making plans. He worked in the science department aboard the ship and was well liked by most everyone.

She rolled onto her back and stared at the fabric canopy of their bed. It had been two months since the attack. The scars on her body had faded -- due mostly to the healing efforts of the *asana*, priests and priestesses, of the Healing Temple -- but her mind hadn't healed. If anything it was getting worse. She rarely left the cabin anymore. When she did, she was twitchy and nervous the moment a stranger got near her. Actually, she couldn't say it was only strangers. It was anyone she did not know well. And since she had not met many people before the attack, that meant most of the ship.

She was tired of the sideways glances and knew most of it was brought on by her own actions. *Sure, one screaming fit because someone touched your arm and everyone thinks you're psycho*, she thought to herself ruefully.

How did someone get past something like that, though? Barik's face floated in her mind. Right after Thea had been brought aboard, it was discovered that someone had raped and tortured several of the human women on the ship. Barik, the rapist, had been trying, in his own twisted way, to prove they were inferior and should not be carrying his race's children. He had selected several women to vent his rage on and was stalking his next victim when he discovered Thea had been marked by his own Gods, snapping his last thread of sanity.

In a fit of rage, he had injected her with venom that had paralyzed most of her body. He had then taken her to an empty cabin where he proceeded to viciously beat her. He was cutting the God-marks from her body when a team of security officers found them and subdued him, but it was too late to save the life of her unborn child. The beating had caused her to miscarry.

She rubbed her hand across her belly. It still felt empty sometimes -- a large, hollow, void where life and warmth had once been. She had barely realized she was pregnant, barely had time to anticipate it when it had been taken from her. She had not even had time to tell her husbands; the first they had known of their child was learning she had miscarried.

Sitting up, she sighed and pushed her heavy red-black mane of hair away from her face. *Okay, Thea, you've put it off as long as you can. Time to see one of the shrinks.* She made a face and moved to change her clothing and com Corvin, the Chief Medical Officer of the ship, to tell him that she was coming.

* * *

She was sweating by the time she arrived at medical and knew that her smile had a decidedly brittle cast to it. Looking around nervously, she quickly scuttled into Corvin's office before he had even finished saying enter. She took a few deep breaths before smiling at him in greeting.

Corvin frowned.

Thea slumped down into a chair. "I know. I look like hell."

He nodded.

Corvin had been her first friend on the ship. He was also her doctor and one of Kyrin's closest friends. He had spent many evenings with them, eating dinner, watching movies, and playing games. She had come to rely on his calming presence and came to him when she needed to talk to someone.

She knew part of it was because he pitched his voice to soothe her. The Ta'e'sha all had the ability to ensnare minds with their voices to varying degrees, but Corvin had trained his own considerable talent to help his patients.

She fiddled with a ragged fingernail. "I'd like to talk to one of the psychiatrists, Corvin. I don't feel comfortable talking to the asana about this right now. They feel too much." Thea's latent psychic abilities were growing quickly, partially due to the trauma of the attack and partially from the stimulation of her husbands' abilities. The Ta'e'sha were a psychic race. As a result, she had times when she could not block out other people's emotions. She didn't have the telepathy common to the Ta'e'sha; her abilities leaned more toward empathy, and possibly mind and soul healing. The asana were going to work with her more after her talents leveled out and there was less chance of her having emotional spikes.

Corvin smiled with relief. "I think that would be a very good idea, Thea. We've all been worried about you. Reba may be free right now; she's the counselor who is working with the other ladies who were attacked. Would you like me to ask if she has time to speak with you? We have given her and the other doctors offices right next door to us."

She nodded gratefully. "That would be great, but if she doesn't have time, I can come back later." She chewed on a fingernail while he contacted Reba and spoke to her quietly.

Several minutes passed before he finished his conversation. "She would like you to stop by now and answer a few questions, and then she'll set up appointments for regular times to see you." He patted her hand gently and shooed her out the door. "Come see me if you need anything else, dear."

Chapter Two

Thea looked around the tastefully appointed waiting area in the center of several private offices. The walls were painted a mellow, soothing cream. The carpeting matched the upholstery on the furniture and was warm shades brown with rusty red accents here and there. The walls had several serene landscapes hung on them. Two women were waiting quietly on chairs.

"May I help you?"

She turned toward the voice. A young human woman was sitting at a receptionist's desk. "I'm here to see Reba. My name is Theadora Auralel; I believe she is expecting me."

The woman nodded. "Of course, Mrs. Auralel. One moment while I com her." She handed Thea a holoreader and stylus. "Could you please fill this out while you wait? She is with another patient at the moment, but will be with you in just a few minutes."

Thea nodded and accepted the reader. She sat down and smiled nervously at the other two women waiting and began to fill out the form. It was a seemingly endless list of questions about her medical history, her family's history, and whether she had ever seen a counselor before.

As time passed, both women were called into other rooms. She finished the form and returned it to the receptionist. Sitting back down, she went back to what was fast becoming her most engrossing hobby: chewing on her thumbnails.

A tall woman with pale, pinched features exited one of the other rooms and strode quickly out of the office.

A few more minutes passed before the door opened again and a slender brunette called Thea's name.

Thea stood and walked to her, smiling nervously.

The woman offered her hand. "Hi, Thea. I'm Reba. Come on in and let's get to know each other."

* * *

Daeshen yawned hugely as he and his husband entered their quarters. "Want to take a nap before dinner?"

Kyrin nodded tiredly. "Sounds good. It's just the three of us tonight, right?"

"I think so," Daeshen replied. "Thea? Are you here, love?" When there was no answer he checked his cerebcom for her location. Both men had become very paranoid about where she was since the attack. He frowned at the response. *What's she doing at Human Medical?* He didn't think she had even known the department was now open. Shrugging it off, he walked into their bedroom and removed his clothes. He could always ask her later.

Kyrin held up a holoreader. "Thea left a note. She'll be gone for a few hours."

Both men crawled onto the bed and soon fell into an exhausted slumber.

Several hours later Thea peeked into the bedroom and checked on them. Seeing they were both dead to the world, she backed out and shut the door securely behind her. She made her way into the kitchen and began preparing dinner, mentally figuring how long they should sleep before they wouldn't be able to sleep tonight. She had decided to sleep in her workroom tonight, so that they could get a decent night's sleep.

As she carefully rinsed sand from vegetables, she reviewed her tentative plans for the marriage veil she was planning for Sya'tia.

Sya'tia was her best friend, and her husbands had been encouraging her to court the other woman. The polygamous marriages common among the Ta'e'sha were still a bit odd to her, but she was coming to accept them. Although, if Sya'tia accepted their proposal, she didn't think she would want to add any more members to their marriage. Their courting habits were very casual by human standards. They spent time doing what friends did. It seemed slightly deceptive to her since you would not know if you were being courted or if the person merely enjoyed spending time with you.

She went back to her plans for the marriage veil. It was the same as offering an engagement ring. A veil was commissioned, then woven in colors the same shades that comprised the person the veil was being offered to. If the proposal was accepted, the person wore the veil until the marriage ceremony. The veil could be worn in any way the person liked.

Thea had been toying with the idea of making the veil pattern based on Celtic knots with a stylized tree in the center, but wasn't sure if she should go with a pattern more traditional to the Ta'e'sha. She didn't want Sya'tia to feel like Thea was pushing her culture down her throat.

Moving the vegetables to the cutting board, she thought about using abstract swirls on a white background. Sya'tia was very pale, so most of the shades of the veil would have just the barest hints of color.

She decided to draw up a few ideas and see which one the men liked best. After tossing the now chopped vegetables into a pan with some melted butter to sauté, she went to wake her husbands up.

Kyrin cracked an eye open as she came in and mumbled a sleepy greeting.

She sat down next to him and rubbed his chest. "Dinner will be ready soon." She patted Daeshen's leg to wake him, grinning when he groaned and rolled over.

Kyrin stood and stretched. "All right." He pulled on a pair of shorts and stretched again.

Thea slipped back out to check dinner while they got ready.

Daeshen came in a few minutes later and stole a quick kiss. He took plates and cutlery out and set the table. "What were you doing in medical today?" he asked casually.

She concentrated on stirring the rice she was making to go with the vegetables. "Um. I went to talk to one of the counselors."

Kyrin strode in with his usual confident energy. "What did you want to talk to the counselor about?" he asked, catching her reply.

Thea ladled the rice into a bowl to avoid looking at them. "The attack." She sprinkled spices over the vegetables.

"I think I need some help dealing with it. And maybe you guys should talk to Reba too. Or go with me a few times."

Silence filled the room.

She chewed on her lip and waited. Anxiety tightened her muscles. She felt them watching her and wondered what they were thinking. She hoped they were willing to try therapy even if they didn't understand her need for it.

"All right," Daeshen said cautiously. "We were thinking about going to the asana, but if you'd feel more comfortable with this, we can do both."

Thea relaxed. "I would rather not go to the asana yet. My control isn't very good and I can feel their emotions. It makes me uncomfortable." She handed Kyrin the bowl of rice. "Kyaness said she'd help me with my shields first, then after that we could deal with the attack if I want to."

The men sat down as she finished scooping the vegetables into another bowl and came to the table. They asked her questions about how human therapy worked as dinner progressed, and she was relieved they were willing to try it and see if it helped. They were a little apprehensive since they didn't know how a nontelepathic person would be able to help, which changed the course of the conversation a little as they talked about the differences.

After dinner the men washed the dishes while Thea got her sketchpad out and started to draw a few rough pictures of some of the ideas she had for the veil. They adjourned to the living room and the men watched a Ta'e'shian video while she worked.

Once the movie was over she showed them both the sketches and asked their opinions. Each sketch was studied carefully.

"I like this one," Daeshen said, pointing at the sketch featuring the tree.

Kyrin hummed softly. He looked over all the sketches again. "I do too. But I also really like this abstract one." He tilted his head.

Thea didn't say anything. She didn't think he was done looking and didn't want to influence him about his choice.

He finally looked up. "Could you combine the two somehow?"

She sat up and thought about it. "Well...I could paint the abstract on the background... Hmm... If I used silk it would be very easy to paint the design around the weave." She picked up her sketchpad again and made a few adjustments to the tree picture. "Like this?"

Daeshen and Kyrin both nodded.

Kyrin smiled with pleasure. "That would be beautiful."

Daeshen agreed enthusiastically.

Thea gathered up her tools. "I'm going to get started on this. I need to make a list of supplies I'll need and ready my loom. I want to make a long veil so she can drape it across her hips while she's working. It won't be in her way if she needs to fight or exercise.

Daeshen kissed her gently. "I'm going to bed. Don't stay up too late."

Kyrin followed him after a more lingering kiss.

* * *

Condezl surveyed his teams. They were good. Very good. Each team was carefully matched to balance both members. Well, for the most part. Humans would have been amazed that they could work together; after all, they were enemies by evolution and instinct.

He nodded to his partner, Myst. It was time.

Myst cawed loudly, as only a raven can, calling the meeting to order.

Eight large cats and eight large birds formed a semicircle around them, and the room quieted.

Condezl stood and stretched from the tips of his ears to the tip of his tail before slowly padding along the line, inspecting each member of his crew.

First up were Lapis and Vons. Lapis was a delicately boned caracal and Vons, a massive, long-suffering raven. He reminded Condezl of an impassive English butler, which perfectly suited Lapis's nit-picking and princess airs.

Next were Orchid and Lyre. Orchid had chosen the form of a margay for this incarnation. She was sweet and calm and generally cooled the hotheads in the group. Her partner, Lyre, was a brilliantly cobalt-shaded blue jay with a bright happy personality.

After them came Twitch and Poe. Condezl occasionally wondered what the Lord and Lady were thinking to put those two together. Twitch, an ocelot, got his nickname due to the fact that he had an eye twitch and saw a conspiracy behind everything. He was currently fixated that alien abductions were fact and now was positive that he was right about everything else as well. Poe didn't help. A morose, depressed, and slightly moth-eaten looking raven, he was always willing to take a pessimistic view of things.

He paused for a moment and winked at Budweiser and his partner, Jorgette. Budweiser was a large, laid-back Maine Coon. His last incarnation was somewhere very southern in the United States, and he retained the accent and mentality in this life as well. Jorgette, a grackle, was the perfect southern lady, which meant she had a sweet tongue like a razor blade. The two of them spent most of their time trying to keep the rest of the teams out of trouble. Condezl was considering making them his seconds, but wanted to see how they handled their missions first.

Moving on, he quickly inspected the next pair, Chimera and Chicory. Chimera flicked an ear at him in lazy acknowledgement. When the Lady had introduced him to the female tiger, he had thought she was going to be a problem with her dominant personality and acidic sense of humor, but he had quickly learned she had no problem taking orders, and was very pleased with her new role. Her partner, Chicory, another blue jay, balanced her well by giving a quick verbal smack anytime she got too mouthy.

The next two teams made him sigh inwardly in resignation. Skids, a marmalade tom and Doober, long-haired black tom. They both stared at him expectantly, positively quivering with the need to get into mischief. Their partners were two crows, Eric and Ash. Both crows were currently wearing sunglasses and had cigarettes hanging from their beaks. Balance was not their strong point. If the cats weren't getting into trouble, they were. He shook his head and moved to the last team.

Shrayne and Cray. He wasn't sure where to put them yet. Shrayne had chosen the form of a clouded leopard and was well-known for handing out fortune cookie advice. She was mystical and deeply spiritual. He wondered if she had spent too many incarnations in a hippie commune. Cray, on the other hand, was very practical and could be counted on to make sure she ate and that the Wonder Twins, as the group was now calling the kittens and crows, didn't bother her too much.

He returned to his post next to Myst. He had chosen the form of a jaguar after the Lord had told him that Thea loved them. It wasn't his first incarnation in this type of body, so he was very comfortable with it.

The Lord and Lady had given them three gifts to help them complete their missions. They would retain those gifts until they asked to be released from their duties. The first gift was that they would not age. The second was the ability to change their size. The third gift was that of illusion, hence the sunglasses and cigarettes.

"*Skids, Doober, are your teams ready for your first mission?*" he asked them quietly, mentally speaking on a thread all could hear.

They both snapped to attention. "*Yes, sir!*" they chorused.

"*Very good. I want you to shrink down and have Ash and Eric fly you to each of the heating cores so you can spray each one. There are fifteen cores and each one turns on every fifteen minutes. Get in, spray, and get out without getting fried.*" He fixed them with a steely eye. "*This is not a video game, you don't get three lives, and I don't want to explain Crisp Kitten à la carte to the Lady. Twitch and Orchid. Your teams will keep watch. Any questions?*"

The other teams nodded in acknowledgement of their duties, and all affirmed they had no questions.

Condezl nodded. "*Good. Get to work!*"

The teams scattered.

It wasn't long before Twitch was sighing as he watched Skids and Doober duck and roll their way down the halls while humming the *Mission: Impossible* theme. Eric and Ash flew wildly above them. They were invisible to everyone but each other. He rubbed his shoulder against Orchid. "*Which set of twins do you guys want, and what did we do to deserve this?*"

Orchid chuffed softly in amusement, making a passing crewman look around in confusion. "*We'll take Skids and Eric. And I was gonna ask you the same question. At least it won't be boring. You guys start at one end and we'll start at the other and meet in the middle. Sing out if you have problems!*"

Twitch nodded his assent and told Doober the plan. Both teams split off at the next intersection.

Fifteen minutes later, Twitch positioned himself at the base of the heating grate. There was warm air issuing from it. Doober and Ash shrank, slipped inside, then waited for Twitch to tell them when to go.

"*Okay. Five minutes to the core, five minutes back. It shuts off in two. Go now and it'll be cool by the time you're there.*"

They were off like a shot, Doober clinging to Ash's back and singing a Beach Boys song with edited lyrics. This mission filled him with glee.

Five minutes later they reached the core. He jumped off Ash's back, enlarged his body, and turned to face away.

Ash backed a distance away. "*Soldier, present arms!*"

Doober lifted his tail.

"*Aim*!"

The cat wiggled his butt.

"*Fire*!"

Doober let free a stream of urine.

He stopped after a moment.

Both of them examined the dripping fixture. It looked like it had gotten a thorough dousing.

Doober shrank and jumped back on Ash. "*Let's go! Twitch says we have eight minutes!*"

An hour and a half later, they returned to the cabin they had commandeered for their use.

"*Water...*" Skids whined plaintively. He headed for a bowl waiting for him, Doober right behind him.

Twitch and Orchid presented themselves to Condezl. "*Mission accomplished, sir. No casualties*" -- their mouths dropped open in feline grins -- "*yet.*"

Condezl nodded, pleased. "*Very good work. Myst and I have a mission; we should be back in half an hour.*"

The teams acknowledged his words and went back to what they were doing: some napping, some planning other missions.

Condezl and Myst flew quietly down the halls until they reached the grate they were looking for. They quickly shrank and followed the vents until they entered a sterile, white room. A quick glance assured them no one was present. The room was filled with cryogenic tubes. Condezl walked along the hall between each row, Myst sitting on his back, until they found what they were looking for.

Barik's tube.

Myst hopped down and Condezl grew to an enormous size, still invisible. He jumped up on his hind legs and rested his paws at the top of the tube, inspecting the face of the man inside. He dug his claws carefully into the plastic casing and dragged them down, scraping long curls of plastic off the case.

Marking him as a dead man. Maybe not now, maybe not soon. But he was a dead man.

Never exchanging a word, they exited as quietly as they had entered.

Chapter Three

Kyrin was going over some of his notes. They were preparing to return to Ta'e in the next few days. Daeshen and his team had just informed him that they'd stored the samples they had room for, and the remaining items on the God List, as his team was calling it, had been sent to the other two ships still in orbit for collection. There was a distinct possibility that another ship would have to be sent out to collect the rest, since it wasn't likely all the items could be collected on the three ships they already had there.

It had caused a mad scramble to gather as many of the samples as possible without completely destroying the schedule for their return to Ta'e.

His nose twitched. He inhaled. There was a faint pungent scent in the air. He ignored it.

If everything is stored by the end of the evening, we should be able to leave within the week. He scribbled out another note on the holoreader, then reached for another reader. This one contained his correspondence not related to the running of the ship. A quick smile graced his face as he scanned several notes. They were thanks from members of the crew and several of their human mates for adding the new entertainments, such as movie theatres, hair salons, and restaurants.

What is that smell? It was growing stronger and decidedly more unpleasant. He pushed back from his chair and entered the main deck. The odor hit him in the face like an enraged woman. "What is that?" Several members of his crew looked at him miserably.

Whist looked up from his work briefly. "No idea, Captain, but maintenance is looking into it. They say complaints have been pouring in for the last hour. It seems to be striking some of the humans strangely. They start laughing hysterically whenever someone mentions it." He looked perplexed.

Kyrin shuddered and commed maintenance to see if they had found the cause yet. After a moment, they responded that they were still looking for it. He requested they turn the air filters up only to be told they were already running at maximum.

The smell grew worse as the day passed. Even the human women no longer found it humorous.

Several hours later he received a com from the maintenance department. "Captain, we have found a substance on the heating cores. We are turning them off one at a time to clean them and see if we can discover what it is. Hopefully, the smell should be gone in an hour or so."

"Let me know as soon as the analysis is complete," Kyrin replied quietly. "And see if you can discover how someone got into the vents to reach the cores."

"Yes, sir."

Chapter Four

Daeshen hummed softly to himself as he carefully packaged the sheaf of papers he had received from the Ta'e'shian deities. They would be placed in a temple once he had finished making copies of the lists. Each page was filled with the ornate script of his people, but it was dry reading. It simply listed the names of different life forms indigenous to the planet Earth.

The papers had been given to him with instructions to gather samples of each. The samples would be given to the scientists on Ta'e to be used to terraform one of the planets in his home system. His team had been scrambling to gather the requested items and catalog the samples that had already been stored by his ship and the others already orbiting the planet. They were hoping to collect as many as possible before they left, but they were running out of room.

One of the human women helping them identify the items on the lists approached him with a frown. "Hey, Daeshen, I think we have a problem." She set a holoreader in front of him. "These items are extinct. I have no clue how we're going to get samples." She leaned down to point at an item. A necklace swung free of the top of her blouse.

Daeshen stared at the necklace, distracted from her questions. It was made of silver and featured a star set inside an ornate circle created by two crescent shapes. It was polished to a high shine and showed signs of long wear. He reached up to touch it. He looked up when she stiffened.

Ruri straightened slowly, her eyes locked with his. She did not speak.

Daeshen studied her, taking in her features again, curious about her reaction. Long, straight black hair swung to the middle of her back and slanted dark eyes marked her of Asian descent. Her slender body stood very still. He tilted his head. "My wife has a necklace similar to that. She doesn't like us to touch it either. Is it a sacred object?"

She relaxed marginally. "Your wife, you say? I would like to meet her, please. This necklace is shaped as a pentagram, a symbol of witches. She could tell you more if you ask her." She blinked slowly. "It would be nice to have another witch to spend time with." Changing the subject, she pointed at the holoreader again. "Please go over this list, and if you have any ideas how we can get living samples of things that have been dead a long time, let me know." She walked away, returning to her workstation, tucking the necklace back into her shirt.

She was very difficult to get along with most of the time. Daeshen had found her to be much angrier about being taken than most of the women. She rarely spoke to anyone and was very curt when she did.

Brow furrowed in confusion, he watched her leave. *What is a witch?* he wondered silently. Deciding to put the matter aside until he got home that evening and could talk to his wife about it, he reached for another sheaf of papers the Gods had given him. The human women had the lists from the first sheets and were moving much faster than his people in cataloging where to find the items. He was going to see if he could identify the contents of the next list since he had barely glanced at it yet.

After perusing the list for a few minutes he let out a heartfelt groan. The others in the room looked up. He held up the list and grimaced. "It's all from Arkaa, people. We need to contact the Council." His head thunked onto the table. Groans sounded around him.

The Arkaana were a race his people had briefly studied before deciding not to contact them. Their culture was matriarchal to an extreme. They had no interest in expanding their few sciences into space travel and were fiercely territorial, yet, not warlike. However, the initial team could not gather very much cultural information, as they were unable to enter the cave systems the Arkaana made their homes in.

The project had been abandoned because of that lack of information. They had managed to get some basic cultural information and the spoken languages, but that was all.

Daeshen sighed again, hoping his ship wouldn't be required for first contact. Then he wondered why the Gods wanted to make a near perfect replica of Arkaa. He sent the information to the head of the science department for review.

* * *

Thea flopped backward onto the bed and stared at the ceiling pensively. She had just returned from a session with Reba, her counselor. They had spent more time discussing her new life than the attack. She wondered if Reba was talking to one of the other counselors about the same things. Did all of the women feel the way she did?

Daeshen came into the room. She watched as he eyed her for a moment before sprawling on his back next to her.

They stared at the ceiling in silence.

After a few minutes, he turned his head and looked at her. "How was your day?" he inquired softly.

She shrugged. "Okay, I guess. I worked for a few hours, pondered how Perry Mason never defends a guilty person for an hour or so, then went to see Reba." Her hand stretched across the bed and she laced her fingers through his. She had introduced Daeshen to old *Perry Mason* reruns a few days ago. He was completely fascinated by them.

He rubbed his thumb along the back of her hand before releasing it and rolling onto his side, propping his head up on his hand. "What do you want to do tonight?"

"I dunno. I'm not really in the mood for a movie. We could go swimming. I wouldn't mind getting some exercise. Or I could see if Sya'tia wants to go jogging instead of swimming. We could pick up dinner in the galley. I don't feel like cooking. Reba says I need to force myself to go out in public. I don't think it would be so bad if you guys were with me." She toyed with a strand of Daeshen's hair; it curled around her fingers, squeezing gently.

He leered at her comically. "Well, I know one way to get some exercise…"

She giggled and pushed him over. "You always want to exercise that way, ya perv." She rolled over and rested her arms and chin on his chest.

He rubbed her back. "It's part of my charm." He smirked.

She wiggled up and kissed his chin. Their sex life had suffered because of the attack. She occasionally panicked when the men leaned over her. It had caused several aborted seduction attempts on their part. Kyrin had ended up with a black eye once when he had tried one of the bondage games they had all enjoyed before the attack. Thea was still mortified she had struck him.

Daeshen threaded his fingers through her hair and gently massaged her scalp. He pulled her closer for a deeper kiss, nibbling gently on her lips.

She pulled away slowly and nuzzled his neck. His hands slid down to rub her lower back. Thea smiled against the skin of his throat and rocked her hips against his. He hardened against her hip eagerly. She slid down his body and opened his suit. His cock pulsed in her hand when she gently freed it from the cloth.

Her tongue flickered quickly across the crown. She pursed her lips and slowly sucked him inside her mouth. His moan of obvious enjoyment was music to her ears and she took more of him. She hummed softly and peeked up at him. His eyes were glazed and his hands fisted in the blanket covering their bed. Her tongue rubbed up and down the firm muscle in her mouth. She drew upward slowly, sucking strongly until she reached the tip.

Her hand slid back inside his clothing and cupped the heavy weight of his jewels. She squeezed them gently as her tongue explored under the sensitive frills spiraling down his glans. They fluttered anxiously against her tongue. Daeshen moved under her, leaning up on his elbows to watch her. He murmured encouragingly. She took him back into her mouth in a smooth motion until he touched the back of her throat.

Thea began to move her lips slowly up and down, letting her teeth graze his sensitive flesh every so often. He moaned and fell back, arching his hips. She felt his balls tighten in her palm. She knew he would not last long. Daeshen loved watching her suck him. She took him as deeply as she could and sucked hard, sealing him in her mouth. Then, she began to hum again, low and deep in her throat. She felt his frills tremble.

With a hoarse shout, he pulled her mouth off of him. His frills popped open and hot, sweet liquid splattered her mouth and cheeks. Thea quickly curled her fingers around him and stroked him as he continued to shoot stream after stream. He shuddered under her and relaxed, the last of his sap flowed sluggishly over her hand. She smiled with pleasure, petting his cock and the frills that still stood out from the tip. He shivered under her caresses. Thea lapped him clean, carefully working her tongue under the rigid frills. He tasted sweet and faintly of licorice.

She rested her chin on his thigh as his frills folded and he panted.

Daeshen looked down at her and laughed softly. "You have cum in your hair again." He laughed again when she just grinned at him. He sat up and pulled her up beside him. "Let's go take a shower and go swimming. I'll com Kyrin and Sya'tia to join us when their shifts end. You could even leave off wearing that flimsy excuse for modesty you call a bikini," he added with a teasing leer.

* * *

Sya'tia watched as Thea lolled on her back in the warm water. "I still say it would be damned uncomfortable! So, it had to have been a man's idea that women wore them!" She rolled onto her back and floated next to her friend.

"Of course it was a man's idea. You honestly think any woman would stick a couple of seashells on her tits and say, 'Hey, this really pinches! I think I'll start a fashion statement!'? Like bras aren't bad enough!"

Sya'tia laughed and exchanged a grin with Kyrin. She looked back at her friend, who now had her eyes closed as she enjoyed the quiet of the recreation area. The place was close to deserted since the galley had just started serving dinner.

She admired the bikini Thea was wearing. It was a pale cream with bright blue swirls. Thea had told her she had "crocheted" it and Sya'tia was thinking about asking her friend to make her one. Although she'd only need the top since her legs became a tail when she was in the water.

Which was where the subject of tonight's discussion had come from. The Ta'e'sha closely resembled the merfolk of human myth and Sya'tia had asked why so many of the pictures featured well-endowed women wearing seashell tops. Thea had muttered something about religious prudes being ashamed of their own bodies.

Sya'tia had pointed out that Thea still wore clothing and was uncomfortable being naked around strangers.

Thea had replied that she was "a product of her environment." Whatever that meant. Sya'tia had changed the subject back to seashells.

With a quiet splash both men dove under the water and disappeared. She felt them pass under her body. She grinned when Thea squeaked and sank under the water. Her friend came back up sputtering and yelling at her husbands.

Sya'tia rolled back over and watched Daeshen swim by. He was a blue streak waving a cream and blue flag.

Thea's bikini bottom.

Thea set off after him. She yelled a few more curses when she couldn't catch him. *Humans are so clumsy in the water*, Sya'tia thought to herself as she watched their antics. Daeshen passed the scrap to Kyrin and tweaked his wife's ass, making her squeak in outrage.

A bit of white in one of the trees caught her gaze. *What is that?* She squinted. A small blue patch floated through the air and landed in the tree as well. It hung up on a branch and waved gently in the breeze. More dots of color floated around. "Uhhhh...Kyrin?" she murmured softly as he passed her.

He paused and looked at her inquiringly.

She nodded toward the tree.

He glanced up and frowned. "What is that?"

"I don't know, but whatever they are they're floating on their own," she replied.

Kyrin swam to the edge and levered himself out of the water, tossing the bikini back to Daeshen absently.

Daeshen stopped to see what Kyrin was doing and Thea snatched her bikini bottom away from him.

Sya'tia levered herself out of the water and murmured the chant to change her tail to legs. Once she was finished she walked to the tree. She snagged a piece of cloth and pulled it free of the branch it hung from.

"What is it?" Kyrin called.

She unfolded the cloth and started to laugh. It was one of the lacy bits of nothing the human women liked to wear under their clothing. "Panties. White lace too. Very sexy." She laughed harder. All the bits of color she had seen were underwear. "I don't know how they got here, but someone seems to have raided the laundry."

Kyrin sighed and commed maintenance. He asked them to come retrieve the clothing and take it back to the laundry before it became common knowledge it was waving from the trees. He fell back on the grass and stared up at the ceiling with its artificial sky. First the substance on the heating cores, now this. He would really like to know who was behind these pranks. So he could strangle them.

A shadow fell over him. He looked back and saw his second in command, Tria. "Hello, Tria, what can I do for you?" he asked neutrally.

She was a stern-faced woman with pale yellow coloring and a stockier build than was common among his people. She sat down next to him and cleared her throat nervously. "I'm sorry to bother you off duty, Kyrin, but I wanted to speak with you about something."

Kyrin sat up and waited. His relationship with his second was strained. They worked well together, but personal beliefs had prevented them from becoming friends. They had decided to not exceed the bounds of their working relationship. As it was they clashed in private on a fairly regular basis over the running of the ship.

Tria smoothed the front of her uniform. "I would like to be transferred planet-side after we return, Kyrin."

Kyrin blinked in shock. He was aware of Daeshen drawing Thea deeper into the lake and of Sya'tia rejoining them. He was grateful for their discreet bid to give them privacy. "Why do you wish to transfer, Tria?"

The woman at his side drew herself up. "I have been offered marriage. But the family does not wish to leave Ta'e."

"I see. I will prepare the papers tomorrow. I will miss having you as my second. For all our differences, you are excellent at your job." He smiled at her. "I wish you joy, and I hope you find the happiness I have."

She gave him a relieved smile. "Thank you." She stood and left quietly.

He was beginning to get many requests like this one. Fertile women were in high demand as mates since the virus's devastating effects. He only hoped the women were careful about accepting offers and that they were being asked for more than their ability to carry children.

*   *   *

Myst cawed happily as she watched the maintenance crew swarm over the trees, pulling down panties and dropping them to the ground. Condezl would be pleased with this bit of work.

It also looked as if their efforts were beginning to bear fruit. The maintenance crew was very irritated. She was sure they were still trying to figure out what the urine was. The twins had almost made themselves sick laughing as they watched the tests.

Chapter Five

Two months later...

"Captain, we have a problem."

Kyrin cringed. He had quickly come to hate that phrase. It was usually followed by a report of an irate passenger or maintenance worker. "Yes, what is it?" He turned to face his second in command.

Tria's lips were compressed in a grim line. "There seems to be bird excrement on all the statuary in the recreation areas. The head of maintenance would like to speak to you privately."

"Send him to my office and com security again. I want to know if they've made any progress finding the cats and birds that seem to be roaming freely on my ship!" Kyrin ground his teeth as he moved toward his office.

His crew had no idea how specimens escaped from the science labs to cause so much havoc! Just a few nights ago he had been awakened by horrible retching noises. It had ended with a very wet sound that made his stomach heave just thinking about it. He had quickly turned on the light to locate the source of the sound, but hadn't found anything.

The next morning he'd "discovered" the cause. In his boot. With his foot. A slimy wet mound of hair and vomit.

Several other people had reported the same discovery in various places. Although the most popular place seemed to be beside beds, where the occupants would put their feet when they got up.

The science department was still swearing that all of the jaguar specimens they had collected were in stasis and accounted for. So, how then did a jaguar hairball end up stuck to his foot?

His wife seemed to find the whole thing very amusing.

The door opened and the head of maintenance strode in with an aggrieved expression.

Kyrin sighed inwardly.

Two hours later he fell into the sitting area with a sigh of pure exhaustion. His wife turned from her film to regard him with bright eyes.

She grinned impishly. "Any more hairballs?"

He glowered at her. "No. Today's fun was bird shit. The asana are pissed because it seems to be on their statues as well as the ones in recreation."

Thea fell back laughing hysterically.

Kyrin growled a curse and stood to leave. "I think you know more than you are saying, wife."

Thea smirked. "How could I possibly know more about this than you do?" She stood and swayed out of the room teasingly.

She stopped at the door and turned to give him a bland smile. "Perhaps you should ask the asana to pray for enlightenment. Maybe your *Lithen* have an idea." She disappeared into the next room.

The asana? What would... His eyes narrowed as he stared at the empty doorway. *She* does *know more than she's telling.* He followed her, determined to get it out of her. He paused when he saw her in the doorway to her workroom. She blew him a kiss just before she shut the door and locked it. *Damn it!*

He glowered at the door for a full minute and considered overriding the lock. Finally, he turned on his heel and marched to the cabin entrance. *Fine, I'll go talk to the asana. Who knows what she thinks that will accomplish?*

* * *

Later that night Thea carefully wiggled her way free of her husbands' arms. She didn't want to wake them. Finally, she was standing beside the bed. She crept into the bathroom and silently dressed. Then, she snagged the bag she had stashed there earlier before sneaking out of the cabin.

She and Ruri were going to try and cast a circle. They had decided to try a small one before the next scheduled full moon on Earth.

Meeting Ruri had done more for her peace of mind than anything else. Knowing she wasn't alone, that there was another witch onboard helped her feel more balanced. Thea was a bit apprehensive by the other woman's caustic personality, though. They had quickly become friends after Daeshen had introduced them, but occasionally Thea left Ruri's company feeling like she'd been rubbed raw with sandpaper.

She paused in the entrance to the recreation area and looked around the darkened area cautiously. It appeared to be deserted. She looked up at the ceiling where the image of two moons glowed gently. How she missed the familiar glow of her home's moon. However, she was coming to appreciate the beauty of new things around her.

A dark shadow popped out from behind a tree and she screeched softly in surprise.

Ruri grinned at her from the shadows. "Gotcha!"

Thea laughed. "Witch!"

"You got it, baby!" The other woman winked and fell into step beside Thea. "I found a great place; it has a ring of trees that kind of remind me of oaks. We should do it there. Did you bring the stuff?"

Thea shook her bag. "Got it right here. Did you find the water?"

Ruri held up a large amber bottle with a cork tightly fitted in the top. "Yup; good thing that weasel I got stuck with brought it."

Thea winced. "How is Kiger's nose?" she asked hesitantly.

Ruri shrugged. "Broken. He better learn to quit putting his hands on me."

"Wow, that's, um, extreme." Thea fumbled for something else to say.

"Not my fault the goof decided to kidnap a kenjutsu instructor," was the blasé reply.

"You're a biologist, Ruri."

"I know, but that's not all I am."

Ruri took the more extreme attitude of the women taken from Earth. She refused to have anything to do with the man who took her and would not acknowledge him as her husband. If he tried to touch her, she usually tried to break something on him. Kiger was on a first name basis with everyone who worked in the medical bays. Ruri swore if he would court her in the traditional Japanese manner she would give him a chance.

Except she hadn't bothered to tell him that.

And he hadn't bothered learning anything about Japan since she was from California.

After hearing that, Thea had come to the conclusion that men were stupid and species didn't change it. But she still didn't approve of the way Ruri treated Kiger. He seemed to be a very nice man.

They reached the area Ruri had described and began setting up for the ceremony.

Thea saw eyes reflecting the light from their candles but didn't draw Ruri's attention to it. She smiled to herself. They would show themselves when they were ready.

Chapter Six

Two weeks later...

Sya'tia paused when the conversation halted and two pairs of eyes speared her. She stepped hesitantly into the room. She relaxed marginally when Thea smiled in welcome. The other woman continued to stare at her with a faintly hostile expression. "Hello, Thea," she said uncertainly.

In the last month Thea had become secretive and wasn't spending as much time with Sya'tia. It hurt more than she had expected. She was sure the reason was glaring at her right now.

Thea closed the book in front of her. "Hey, Sya, this is my friend Ruri. Ruri, this is my best friend, Sya'tia."

Sya'tia nodded. The intensity of Ruri's glare eased but did not completely fade. "Hello, Ruri, nice to meet you." She sat down beside Thea and looked at the cover of the book. It was old and covered with scarred leather. There was no title or markings on the cover. "What's this?"

The human women exchanged a glance. Sya'tia didn't react when Ruri shook her head slightly. She watched Thea's features tighten and her eyes narrow.

"This is not the Middle Ages. There will not be burnings, Ruri."

Sya'tia blinked, mystified. She had no idea what they were talking about.

"She's not one of us, Thea."

Sya'tia felt her heart wilt slightly. Those words hurt, even from a stranger. She was always "not one of us." She had been born with features that most of her people considered birth defects. And while you could say many great things about her people and her culture, they were not a race that readily accepted someone born looking like a throwback. Even though her features were like those in the carvings and artwork depicting their own gods and goddesses.

Thea's shoulders squared. "She is part of me. And I'm not hiding." She pushed the book toward Sya'tia. "This is a Book of Shadows, Sya. It's been passed down in my family for eight generations. It contains the spells and rituals of my religion."

Sya'tia smiled brilliantly at her friend. "I see." She looked down at the book, not wanting her friend to see the tears pooling in her eyes at Thea's words. This small woman beside her had never made her feel like a freak and had always had a kind word or hug for her. She didn't look up as Ruri slammed away from the table. "Why is it called a Book of Shadows?" she asked softly.

Thea leaned back in her chair. "Well, Ruri and I are witches, and hundreds of years ago witches were hunted down and killed by members of other religions. As a result the witches went into hiding. We had to practice in the shadows, where no one would find us."

Sya'tia ran her finger over the soft leather. "I see." She looked up at Ruri. "Hiding is a habit now?" she asked the other woman quietly.

Ruri nodded slowly. "For some of us." She shot a glare at Thea.

"Then I will leave you to your shadows." She stood and pressed a kiss onto Thea's cheek. "Jogging and a horror movie tonight, love?"

Thea smiled and nodded. "It's your night to bring dinner."

Sya'tia grinned. "Okay, see you in a few hours." She strolled out, feeling much lighter.

The moment the door closed Ruri spun and snarled at Thea, "Where the hell do you get off? You had no right to tell her that!"

Thea straightened and stared long and hard at Ruri. "You have no right to tell me who I can and cannot tell. I don't care where you come from, or what you were before you came here. So, don't pull that alpha bitch bullshit on me." She crossed her arms under her breasts and stared at her friend.

Ruri looked up at the ceiling for a minute then sighed. "We don't know how these people will react to us. Sure, the Ta'e'sha may be accepting, but what about the other women from home? Are you willing to let it become common knowledge that we are witches?"

Thea nodded slowly. "I am willing to take that risk. Would you like to know why?"

The other woman nodded slowly.

"Because Kyrin and Daeshen ask me questions and then leave it alone. They don't try to convert me. Because none of the other women we've met seem to care, they are too busy with their own lives." Thea smiled slightly. "Don't make problems that aren't here. If someone has a problem with us, we'll deal with it as it arises. However, I, for one, plan on living my life, not worrying about what someone else is going to think."

"Whatever. Are we still doing circle this weekend?"

Thea nodded.

Ruri squared her shoulders. "Fine. I'll see you then," she grumbled and promptly left.

Thea sighed and stroked her hand over the old leather covering the book. The more she got to know Ruri the less she liked the woman's attitude. Ruri seemed to carry a chip on her shoulder about *everything*. The smallest thing would set her off and she had no tolerance for the Ta'e'shian people. Any of them. She treated Kyrin and Daeshen with barely veiled contempt most of the time and was downright abusive to almost everyone else.

Thea was starting to get tired of it. She had enough things going on in her life she needed to deal with without listening to someone spew poison every time she disagreed with her.

She leaned back in her chair. "Blah, I'm going to have a talk with Ruri. I can't deal with her and I'm not going to keep swallowing it every time she treats people badly," she muttered to herself. "It's the same as saying it's okay."

She pushed away from the table, suddenly feeling the need to be held by her husbands.

* * *

Condezl and Shrayne watched silently. They had decided to keep an eye on Thea and Ruri for a while to see how they interacted. Shrayne wanted to see how they dealt with each other.

"*This is going to be interesting,*" Condezl sent to the other cat. "*They could easily end up enemies. It's starting already. Thea will put up with Ruri's attitude for only so long. Especially when that attitude starts to affect her family.*"

Shrayne nodded pensively, staring at something that wasn't there. "*Ruri is very discordant. That is why I chose her.*" The smaller cat's mental voice floated in Condezl's head like smoke on still air. "*She is not at peace within herself and as such will not find peace outside herself. Discord has become so natural to her she spreads it without thought. I will help her in this.*" She curled her front legs under her chest and blinked slowly at Condezl. "*The others come this moon?*"

"*Yes.*"

"*You must impress upon the Twins the graveness of the evening.*"

Condezl chuffed softly with amusement. "*I'm leaving that to Chimera and Chicory.*"

* * *

Kyrin popped his head into Thea's workroom. "Ready to go jogging?"

Thea turned and smiled brightly. "Yup, but go grab Daeshen, please. I finished the veil."

Kyrin grinned and went to find his husband. They were both curious to see the finished product since Thea had refused to let anyone see it before it was done.

He found Daeshen digging under their bed for something. Kyrin paused for a moment to admire the view. His firm ass wiggled a bit before Daeshen scooted back out.

Daeshen frowned at the balls of yarn in his hands.

"What are those doing under there?" Kyrin asked.

"Dunno, maybe Thea dropped them. They looked like something has been chewing on them, though."

Kyrin stole a quick kiss. "Come on. Thea finished the veil; she wants to show it to us."

Daeshen's eyes lit up with excitement. They quickly went to see the eagerly awaited item.

When they arrived at the door, Thea was straightening the last edge of the veil. The men gathered close to see. Kyrin moved to the side when Thea wiggled between them and slid her arms around their waists.

The veil was six feet long and two feet wide. The weave was strong and precise, the colors perfectly suited to Sya'tia's pale coloring. It almost appeared to glow in the bright light. Pale swirls of color accented the pure white silk and the pastel browns and greens of the tree covering the center of the veil. More white silk edged the veil with delicate crocheted seashells shot through with palest blue.

Daeshen traced a finger along the design woven into the edges of the silk. "What is this writing?"

Thea leaned against him. "Those are runes for love, security, and protection."

"It's beautiful, love." Kyrin pressed a kiss on the top of Thea's head.

"Do you think she'll like it?" she asked anxiously.

Daeshen nodded happily. "She's going to be stunned, darling. It's wonderful, better than the veils my father gave my mothers. Your work is going to be in high demand."

Kyrin watched her carefully roll the fabric into a neat bundle. "When would you like to present it to her?" He caught a lock of her hair and tugged gently, bringing her attention back to him after she finished.

"I dunno. What do you think?" She peered up at him and leaned against his chest.

Kyrin rubbed his hands up and down her back while he thought about it. "After dinner?"

"Okay," she replied softly.

Half an hour later they'd met Sya'tia and were jogging through the paths in the recreation area. Kyrin watched the smooth play of muscle under the women's clothing. Thea had been doing much better since she had started going to see the therapists. Her nightmares had diminished and she seemed to be more at ease around people. He wished the therapy were helping him as well. It was an interesting experience but seemed much slower than working with the asana. He had talked to Thea last night and she finally felt ready to let them help her as well. He'd sent off a com to Kyaness to ask if she could set up an appointment for them to see her.

He had felt something ease in his chest when she had agreed to talk to Kyaness. Kyrin hadn't been aware of how hard it was to talk to the human therapists until that moment. For some reason it had seemed so much harder to speak the words aloud than to let an asana pull them from his mind.

Daeshen nudged him as they jogged. He looked over at his husband with an inquiring expression. Daeshen leered and wiggled his eyebrows at the women's asses. Kyrin grinned and winked.

They jogged around a curve and began to slow as they finished the final loop of their jog. He wasn't really thrilled with Thea's preferred choice of exercise, but she didn't really like trying to swim with them. She had commented it was like a mouse trying to keep up with a horse.

As they slowed to a stop and began walking to cool down, several people waved and called greetings. He watched his wife tense, but smile gamely and return the friendly remarks. For once she wasn't shaking by the time they were walking out.

Maybe the sessions with Reba were helping more than he had realized.

They stopped by Sya'tia's cabin to help her carry the food she had prepared for dinner that evening. He looked around curiously; it wasn't often that he and Daeshen came in.

The rooms were neat and bare. Very few personal items were visible other than some pictures of her family and some mementos. His wife followed Sya'tia into the bathroom to rinse her face while Sya'tia took a quick shower. He and Daeshen wandered into the living area to wait.

The walls were light blue and Ta'e'shian weapons were displayed in strategic places. It looked like she was ready for an invasion. Now he had a better idea what Thea had meant when she had said it looked like Sya'tia lived in a constant state of paranoia.

"*Our cabin is going to look like an armory after Sya'tia moves in,*" Daeshen sent to him on a private thread, echoing Kyrin's thoughts. "*Well, if she accepts us.*"

* * *

Sya'tia eyed her friends as they finished clearing the soiled dishes from the table. All evening they had been casting secretive little smiles at each other and now she was beyond curious about what was going on in their heads. It was obvious they were up to something. She shrugged mentally. They would tell her or they wouldn't. Or she'd pry it out of Thea later.

They shooed her out of the kitchen claiming they weren't going to worry about washing the dishes.

"Could you start the movie, Sya? We'll be in there in just a minute or two," Thea asked with a sweet smile.

"Sure." She meandered into the living area and settled into the bowl-shaped couch that was set into the middle of the floor and clicked the controls set into the table resting in the center of the seating area. A large screen shimmered into view on the far wall. She pondered her choices for a bit before finally settling on something about small evil creatures that multiplied when water is thrown on them.

Humans had a rather sick fascination with death and dismemberment, she decided. How they could find those movies about knife wielding maniacs so entertaining she didn't know. They seemed to only highlight the vicious side of their nature. She had noticed that Thea wasn't watching as many since she had been attacked. Even some of the movies that had been her favorites scared her now.

* * *

"You do it."

"No, it's your duty."

"Is not."

"Yes, it is."

Thea sighed in frustration and blew a lock of hair out of her eyes. She glared up at him. "I want you to do it."

Kyrin grinned and shook his head.

Daeshen was sprawled across the bed, watching their antics. He propped his head up on a hand and hummed to himself, wondering how long they were going to argue. Not that it would do any good. Thea was bound to lose since it was custom for the first wife of a mated set to offer the veil to another woman. Likewise, if they decided to ask another man to join them, Kyrin would have to offer the veil. If a member of the opposite sex offered the veil it meant that the husband or wife who had refused to do so was accepting the proposal and inclusion of another member under duress. Such proposals were usually refused.

As he watched, Kyrin bent down and kissed Thea. He slowly deepened the kiss until she collapsed against his chest and moaned into his mouth. Daeshen smirked. They had discovered that she was rather pliant after a kiss like that and they both used it to their advantage when they had annoyed her.

Kyrin slowly lifted his mouth from hers. "You have to do it, love," he whispered.

She nodded with a dazed expression.

Daeshen snickered.

Kyrin picked up the veil and pressed it into Thea's hands.

Her expression cleared as she looked at the silk. "That wasn't fair," she grumbled. Her fingers nervously smoothed the cloth. She took a deep breath and turned to leave the room.

Daeshen rolled off the bed and followed her, lacing his fingers with Kyrin's. He was just as nervous as she was, but he didn't want her to know that.

Sya'tia looked up when she heard them come in. She smiled brightly. "Ready to watch the movie?" Her smiled faded as she took in their nervous expressions. Thea's normally healthy color had a faintly gray cast to it. "What's wrong?"

Thea fidgeted.

Sya'tia stood up, beginning to feel alarmed.

Thea stopped in front of her and looked back at the men. They nodded.

She held out a small bundle of cloth. "Sya'tia, will you marry us?" she blurted out in a rush.

Sya'tia froze. Her mind scrabbled franticly as she stared at the cloth being offered to her. She felt the blood leave her face in a cold rush, only to return hotly. Never in her wildest dreams had she thought this would happen. She had resigned herself to the belief that the only marriage proposal she would ever receive would have been out of pity.

Her fingers itched to snatch the veil.

She held herself back and stared deeply into Thea's gray eyes. The hope and nervousness there struck her. Her heart tightened. There was no pity there. She looked up at Kyrin and Daeshen, taking in how tightly they held each other's hands. Their eyes held the same emotions.

She smiled slowly. Her hands reached for the precious veil. "Yes, I would be honored to join your family." Her fingers tingled as they stroked the smooth cloth. It was unlike anything she had ever felt. Tears welled in her eyes.

Thea squealed and threw her arms around Sya'tia, hugging her tightly. She giggled and returned the hug. Warm emotion squeezed her heart. Thea leaned back, her face serious again.

The smaller woman stood up on tiptoe and gently pressed a soft kiss against Sya'tia's mouth. It was over as soon as it began.

Sya'tia licked her lips.

Thea stepped back.

Both men came forward for their own, more generous, kisses.

After they had settled closely together on the couch, Thea cuddled against her side, she slowly unfolded the veil.

"Oh. Oh my," she murmured softly, taking in the delicate threads and colors. "It's so beautiful." Her hands caressed it gently. Her mind reeled again. *She was getting married!*

"I made it long enough for you to wear however you want," Thea piped up anxiously. She pointed out different features of the cloth. "It's very strong too. It's hard to rip or tear good silk."

Sya'tia admired the design. The veil was the finest she had ever seen. Her sisters would be so jealous! She couldn't wait to show them! The minute she got back to her cabin she was going to send her family a communication and let them know. She stood and carefully draped the veil around her hips and tied an artful knot that caused the remaining length to cascade down her hip and leg. It shone like a glistening gem against the black matte fabric of her jumpsuit.

Thea reached out and carefully fanned and pleated the silk over Sya'tia's hip. "There. It looks great!" She beamed.

Sya'tia laughed happily. It did look good. Thea had measured the length almost perfectly. It fell a few inches below her knee. She stroked the silk, loving the feel of it against her fingers.

She looked up hesitantly and asked, "When would you like me to move my things?"

They all looked at Kyrin.

He coughed. "Um, tomorrow? Daeshen and I can help after our shift ends. Thea can help you pack during the day. Tomorrow is your free day, isn't it?"

She nodded happily. "I have to go now; I want to com my family." She kissed each of them again and scampered out.

Kyrin blinked after her. "That wasn't quite how I had expected the evening to end," he said ruefully.

Thea grinned and Daeshen laughed softly.

"Well, we don't always get what we want, my love," Thea said fondly, pressing a kiss onto his chin.

He growled softly and pulled her down into his lap and pressed sloppy kisses all over her neck while she laughed and tried to squirm free. "You'll just have to make up for it, wife."

He winked at Daeshen, who was watching them with bright eyes.

Daeshen leaned over and tickled Thea's belly. "Can I help?" he asked with a wicked grin and hot eyes.

Kyrin's body warmed at the sensual promise in that look. "Oh, yes, be my guest," he murmured.

Chapter Seven

Thea peered into Sya'tia's cabin. The door had opened but her friend was nowhere in sight. She strolled into the living area. Hover lifts were scattered everywhere, most only half full.

"Sya?" she called.

"In here," came the reply from the bedroom.

She followed the sound of Sya'tia's voice and found the other woman folding clothing and packing it into boxes. "Hey, good morning." Sya'tia blew her a kiss without replying and continued pulling clothes out of the closet.

She was dressed in her usual uniform of matte black. The veil was wrapped around her waist again, but the ends had been crisscrossed around her leg and secured at her knee to keep it out of the way. It was rather striking. Thea made a note to try something similar with longer strips of fabric.

"Want some help?" she asked, coming to a stop beside the taller woman.

Sya'tia's black eyes gleamed with pleasure. "Sure, you can fold these. I'm almost done in here." She handed Thea an armful of clothing.

Thea laughed softly. "We need to get you some clothes with color, love," she said looking at all the black jumpsuits. "Don't you own anything besides jumpsuits?"

Sya'tia smirked. "Yes, I own something besides jumpsuits." She pulled out a few more sets of clothing. "I have my formal uniforms too." She giggled when Thea started laughing.

"Well, that's okay then, isn't it?" Thea giggled again. "Seriously, I can make you some."

They continued to pack the clothes in companionable silence. After they finished with the clothes they moved into the kitchen and went through the cabinets and drawers. Sya'tia wasn't taking everything with her. A good portion would stay in the cabin for the next occupant. Most of the items she was leaving were ship's property and it was easier to leave it than have the crew haul it out, only to have to haul it back in when the next person moved in.

Several hours later Thea was wrapping cloth around the last of Sya'tia's weapons when she felt arms slide around her waist. She jumped when soft lips feathered down the side of her neck. She turned and met Sya'tia's eyes. "Uhhhh…"

She felt Sya'tia go still.

"You don't want me?" Her arms dropped from Thea's waist.

Thea winced inwardly at the hurt in her betrothed's voice. She pulled Sya'tia's arms around her again. "It's not that. I do want you." She blushed hotly. "But I've never been with anyone other than Kyrin and Daeshen."

Sya'tia thought about that for a moment, watching Thea somberly. "Oh." She relaxed again and slowly drew Thea toward her. "Do you want me to stop?"

Thea stared owlishly up at her and slowly shook her head. "No."

Sya'tia slowly bent her head and licked Thea's lower lip. She tilted her head and pressed closer to Thea's soft form, enjoying the feel of the other woman's breasts pressing against her.

Thea's mouth tentatively opened under hers. Sya'tia deepened the kiss. She could feel the smaller woman trembling slightly and responded by gently stroking her back. It was a humbling feeling to know Thea had never been with another woman and that she trusted her so much. She had confided to Sya'tia that she was having trouble being intimate with her husbands right after the attack, but that it was gradually getting better.

She marveled at Thea's bravery to be willing to take another person into her life, and into her bed and heart, after what had happened to her.

She gently led Thea back into the bedroom, stealing soft kisses. Her hands went to the buttons on Thea's slacks and she slowly pulled them free. Their gazes stayed locked together as Thea's hands began to undo the fastenings on Sya'tia's jumpsuit.

She steadied the smaller woman as she stepped out of the pants now pooling around her ankles. Sliding her hands under Thea's shirt, she carefully peeled it up and over her head before tossing it to the side. She had to smile at the lacey bits of nothing Thea wore under her clothes. Her creamy white skin played peek-a-boo with the light blue lace. It was a sensual feast for the eyes.

Sya'tia ran her hands down Thea's sides and hips. "You are beautiful," she murmured, bending to kiss Thea again.

Thea pressed herself closer, lifting her head to accept the kiss. It was so different from being kissed by her husbands. It was softer, but just as sweet. She pushed the jumpsuit off Sya'tia's shoulders and it fell to her hips, catching at the last closure. The feel of Sya'tia's skin against hers was like rolling naked on silk sheets. It flooded her mind and made her burn.

Her hands settled nervously on Sya'tia's hips, not really knowing where else she should put them. She stroked the smooth skin anxiously. Sya'tia's fingers danced lightly up and down her ribs, making Thea shiver. Goose bumps rippled to the surface everywhere she touched Thea's sensitive skin. "Oh, that feels nice," she murmured against those soft lips.

Sya'tia's lips curved against hers for a moment before they opened. Her tongue made a gentle foray into Thea's mouth, stroking slowly. Strong hands slipped around Thea's back and flipped the catch to her bra. The lacey confection popped loose and hung on her shoulders, barely covering her breasts. Sya'tia's hand slid down her shoulders, pushing the pretty scrap off.

Thea let it drop to the floor, her mouth still caught by the other woman's. Each kiss was like a drug clouding her senses. Her hands cupped the taller woman's face. She stood on tiptoe and nipped Sya'tia's lower lip. She rubbed her nose against hers and smiled into Sya'tia's black eyes.

Arousal curled through her body, slow and languid. It was like standing before a fire on a cold winter day, gentle and steady. Her hands stroked down Sya'tia's throat, over her collarbones, and brushed teasingly across the tops of her breasts. Her caresses were hesitant and exploratory. Her thumbs timidly stroked Sya'tia's nipples. She paused uncertainly when Sya'tia drew in a sharp breath and arched into the touch. Becoming bolder, she brushed the hard nubs again.

Sya'tia's mouth traveled down her neck as she hummed her approval deep in her throat. Thea tilted her head back, enjoying the sensation. Her own nipples hardened into tight peaks. She relaxed, her hands now cupping the firm, smooth globes under her fingers. She began to knead them gently, exploring the soft silky flesh. It was so different from anything she had felt before. Her husbands were all rock hard muscle. Sya'tia was firm, yet soft, and her skin had the texture of velvet. Her hands slid down and pushed at the jumpsuit, where it rested at Sya'tia's hips. She fumbled with the closure until it finally snapped loose, and she pushed the garment and the veil free. It fell to her feet and Sya'tia kicked it away.

Sya'tia pushed her gently toward the bed. Her pale body glimmered gently in the light of the room as she followed Thea's slow progress backward. Thea jumped a little when she felt the bed hit the back of her knees. She trembled when Sya'tia's fingers slid down to her hips and began to press her panties off. Her gaze locked with Sya'tia's, seeking reassurance.

The other woman responded by kissing Thea's nose. "It's okay, love. Relax." She finished removing the last bit of Thea's clothing.

Thea cuddled close when Sya'tia's arms curved around her. She felt completely out of her depth. Being with Sya'tia carried the feeling of danger and the forbidden. Never in her wildest dreams had she thought she would be in this position. It felt foreign and yet just exactly where she was supposed to be.

She pulled away and sat on the bed, looking up at Sya'tia. She watched as Sya'tia placed one knee on the bed and leaned over her. She shivered as the other woman's hand pressed against her shoulder. Thea didn't resist as Sya'tia pushed her back and then slid down beside her.

Thea rolled onto her side and faced Sya'tia. Their hands gently stroked each other, learning each other's bodies. Their gazes locked solemnly, taking their time. There would never be another first time. Thea was deeply aware of how careful Sya'tia was being. She knew the other woman was worried about scaring her.

She leaned onto her shoulder and kissed Sya'tia's throat. She pressed against Sya'tia's shoulder and leaned over her. Her lips trailed over Sya'tia's collarbone and came to a stop over the upper curve of her breast. Peeking up, she watched Sya'tia's face as her tongue lapped tentatively across a taut nipple. When Sya'tia drew in a soft breath, her lips closed over it and she sucked it slowly into her mouth.

Thea's eyelids fluttered shut and she kneaded the soft flesh gently as she nursed the tender morsel in her mouth. She wiggled a bit closer, pressing their bodies tighter together. Her hips nudged Sya'tia's. Moist heat pulsed in her core. She moaned around Sya'tia's breast as hands stroked up and down her back and squeezed her butt gently.

Sya'tia's eyes fluttered open. She looked down at Thea. Her dark hair was spread over Sya'tia's stomach like a silky blanket. She hummed softly with pleasure. Unbidden, she began to sing one of the ancient mating songs of her species. Her hands stroked Thea's hair as the smaller woman stilled. Her suckling lips stopped and she looked up at Sya'tia with faintly glazed eyes.

A faint flush of pink warmed her cheeks as she bent her head to take Sya'tia's nipple back into the moist warmth of her mouth. Her hand trailed over Sya'tia's hip, making her shiver at the tickle. The exploring hand pressed against the inside of her thigh. She obligingly parted her legs, still singing softly.

A moment later the song came to a stuttering halt as Thea's fingers traced the seam to Sya'tia's hot core. She moaned as they parted the damp folds and teased the aching tip of her clit. Those fingers quickly became slick with Sya'tia's arousal and began to explore the moist skin. She arched into the delicate touches. Her hands bunched in Thea's hair and she gently tugged the other woman up for a kiss. Her tongue pressed aggressively into Thea's mouth, plundering the sweet tasted of her betrothed.

Their mouths moved feverishly against one another's. Wet tongues twined and danced together anxiously. Sya'tia broke the kiss with a gasp as Thea pressed two fingers into her hot, wet depths. Her hips rolled easily as they began to thrust slowly in and out.

She pushed Thea away, shivering as Thea's fingers withdrew from her warm body. She slid her thigh between Thea's, pressed it firmly against Thea's wet sex, and began to rock her leg back and forth. She kissed her gently as soft moans began to fill the air. The wet scent of their bodies perfumed the chamber.

Sya'tia pressed her mouth against Thea's throat and drew strongly on her soft, fragrant skin as she rocked her love closer to orgasm. She reveled in the small sounds of enjoyment Thea made. Her own arousal grew as Thea's moisture slicked her leg and the soft lips parted, allowing Thea's clit to rub directly against her leg.

Thea's leg curled over Sya'tia's hip as she rocked her body in time to Sya'tia's movements. She twisted and ground as the heat in her loins built. Her mind felt fuzzy with desire. When Sya'tia had begun to sing, her inhibitions had melted away, leaving only the fierce need to be with this woman. The doubts and nervousness had left her. Every fantasy she had ever had about Sya'tia came roaring to the surface of her thoughts.

A faint sting jerked her mind back to the woman making love with her. She watched with glazed eyes as Sya'tia's fangs scraped across the sensitive skin on her breast. She had no fear that she would be bitten, and the sensation of pain heightened her pleasure. She gasped as Sya'tia's hair curled around her breasts and squeezed gently, the tips lazily stroking her nipples.

Sya'tia's motions picked up speed as she ground herself against Thea's leg, where it had slipped between her thighs and was now stroking her as she stroked Thea. They both moaned with mutual enjoyment. Small bursts of pleasure began to radiate from her damp center. Thea twisted and arched against her. Sya'tia screamed as Thea's fingers clenched on her hips, and they both bucked as their orgasms cascaded through their bodies.

Moments passed as they continued to strain, their bodies racked with shivers. At last, they stilled.

Sya'tia rested her forehead against Thea's and panted softly. The smaller woman trembled and purred softly with satisfaction. Sya'tia sighed with relief as Thea's fingers relaxed their death grip on her hips. Her hair slowly unwound from Thea's breasts and curled lazily around both of them, cocooning them in its gently massaging grasp.

She cuddled Thea closer, pressing small kisses along her jaw as their eyes drifted closed and they fell asleep in each other's arms.

Chapter Eight

Somewhere else...

Gaia lounged upside down in her husband's easy chair. Her feet rested over the edge of the backrest and her head hung off the end of the seat. She gnawed on the strawberry held daintily in her fingers. It was perfectly ripe and sweet. She loved them. Truly, they were one of the Great One's greatest creations. She took another bite, sucking up the juice that oozed as her teeth sank into the succulent morsel.

She was watching *Logan's Run*. The dialogue blared from nonexistent speakers. Skye was off doing God-type stuff. She was taking a break. Even a Goddess had to pause and admire a young Michael York running around in strategically ripped, skintight clothing.

A figure shimmered between her and the movie as Logan began screaming, "You don't have to die!" enthusiastically.

She glowered at the interruption. It wasn't often she hid away for a bit and watched TV.

Samonan, Ta'e'shian Goddess of Spirit and Soul Renewal, glared down at her. Her red fishlike tail flicked irritably. Her whole form was shades of red -- blood red hair and sparkling ruby scales. Her skin was a pale, almost pink, shade.

Gaia took another long sucking bite of her strawberry. "Got a problem?" she mumbled around the fruit.

Samonan practically vibrated with outrage. "Those demon-spawned birds of yours *shit* all over my statuary!" she bellowed. Her hair writhed angrily around her like strands of blood. Her garnet eyes shot sparks.

Unimpressed, Gaia finished her snack and licked the juice from her fingers. "Uh huh." She rolled around to sit upright and took a sip of the drink she had sitting on the table next to her. The movie faded out. "Pretty creative way to stir up your bratty kids, wasn't it?"

The other Goddess growled. "You sanctioned it?"

"Nope, but, then, I don't control their every move," was the blasé reply.

Samonan glowered at her sister-Goddess and loomed over her. "Just what did you tell them, then?"

Gaia shrugged. "We told them to drive your children nuts. They have become very arrogant and We didn't see you and yours doing anything about it." She stood up and poked Samonan in the chest. "What, you thought We were going to wring Our hands while Our daughters had nervous breakdowns? That your children can do anything they want and damn the consequences? It doesn't work like that and you know it!"

The chair disappeared as Gaia paced in front of Samonan. "You're just lucky it was Us who decided to cause mischief and not some of the others. So far they haven't paid much attention to what's going on, but what happens if they do? You had better hope Kali doesn't decide to take an interest! You and your children have been left blissfully alone for a very long time."

Samonan opened her mouth then closed it, a thoughtful expression crossing her face. Her hair slowed. She tilted her head to the side as if listening to a voice only she could hear.

Gaia waited patiently.

After a few minutes Samonan's eyes refocused on Gaia. "I see." Her red hair twisted itself up into a tail. "Perhaps you are right. We have coddled Our children. I will speak to the others."

Gaia nodded and sighed as the other Goddess faded from sight. She couldn't really blame the children. They had never had to go on faith alone as Her children had. There was much about oneself that a person learned in the contemplation of faith. Some of it was lost when belief became fact.

She flopped down in the chair that reappeared under her. Maybe Her brothers and sisters would think about it now.

* * *

Daeshen laughed when several boxes were delivered to their quarters. It looked like Sya'tia and Thea hadn't wasted any time packing. He directed the maintenance crew to place them in one of the empty rooms until they could be unpacked.

At least it wasn't an avalanche of belongings. Unlike when Thea's stuff had arrived. He wondered briefly where they were. He checked his com for the time. Kyrin would be home soon. He doubted the women had thought about dinner so he ordered something from the galley. If they did anything tonight, it would probably be unpacking.

After a half hour of waiting, he decided to see how much was left to move and headed for Sya'tia's cabin. A note he had received earlier had informed him Sya'tia had keyed the three of them to be able to enter her quarters whenever they wanted.

He took a quick look through the rooms and didn't see either one of them. Finally he decided to check the bedroom when neither of them responded to his soft calls. He came to a stop in the doorway and smiled slowly.

The women were curled tightly together on the bed, sound asleep. Sya'tia's arms and hair were wrapped around them protectively. A pure black eye popped open when he stepped quietly into the room. She sent him a blissful smile and adjusted her hold on Thea, who was still sleeping. He settled on the bed beside her and stroked her back.

He admired their nude bodies. It was a beautiful picture. Thea's dark hair was tangled in Sya'tia's white locks. The pale icy blue of Sya'tia's skin drew out the warm rosy hue of Thea's. The soft shimmer of Thea's God-marks peeked out from between their entwined hair. Daeshen leaned over and kissed Sya'tia, who murmured softly with pleasure. "I think I can guess what you two have been doing this afternoon," he whispered teasingly.

She smiled shyly. "How was your day?" she asked softly, her hands gently roaming over Thea's sleeping form. A few strands of her hair separated from the rest and stretched up to caress Daeshen's face.

He smiled down at her and stroked her cheek. "It was good, better now. I'm going to take some of the boxes over to our quarters. Kyrin should be off soon. Join us when she wakes up." He laid a smacking kiss on her lips before leaving.

He strolled out with a happy smile and quickly loaded a hover lift with boxes. Anticipation curled through his body; he was feeling very good about himself and his family. It was a quiet pleasure, but no less satisfying. Things were coming together very nicely. He and Kyrin had made the right decision when they had decided to wait for the right mates.

It wasn't something he thought about often, but over the years there had been several offers made to them. But Daeshen had always felt it wasn't time and had convinced Kyrin to wait. The other man had been a bit impatient with the delays. He was very eager to start a family, but he had understood that if Daeshen was uncomfortable there would be discord in the marriage.

There was no such thing as divorce in their culture. Mating was for life, and should be a carefully made decision.

The moment he had seen Thea he had known. She was the one. Adding Sya'tia to their unit was just as wonderful. He had always had a secret fascination with the exotic woman. Seeing her always sent a small thrill of danger through him. He had a little fantasy about her that he had never told anyone about. Not even Kyrin.

He smiled to himself, thinking about Sya'tia and Kyrin. Both were unusually aggressive for his race. Strong and self-assured, they were bound to clash over the care of their family. He was looking forward to the sparks. A vision of Sya'tia tying Kyrin up to make him listen to her sent a flutter of warmth through his groin. Oh yes, it was going to be fun being married to both. He and Thea could place bets when the fireworks started.

* * *

Thea peeked over Daeshen's shoulder. Both men were sleeping deeply. She slipped one leg over his hips and eased out of the bed, freezing when he murmured softly in his sleep and wiggled against her thigh. After a moment he stilled again.

She carefully slipped into the bathroom and gathered her bag before leaving their quarters. She knew she would have to eventually tell her husbands what she was doing. She didn't really want them to wake up in the middle of the night and worry about where she was.

She hummed happily to herself as she strolled down the corridor in a leisurely fashion. The men had been a bit disappointed when Sya'tia had gone back to her quarters after spending the evening with them. She had claimed she wanted to get a bit more packing done before going to bed since she was scheduled to work for the next few days.

Her nap earlier with Sya'tia had refreshed her so she wasn't especially tired tonight. It was a nice change from constantly feeling exhausted. Her sleeping habits were slowly getting back on track as she continued her therapy sessions with Reba. They were going to begin seeing Kyaness within the next few days as well. She wasn't sure how she felt about that yet. But could she really say no when her husbands had been so willing to try it her way? It didn't seem fair to them to continue to see Reba when it wasn't helping them as much as it was her. Maybe trying both methods would have greater results.

She reached the recreation area. The artificial sky was dark and shadows were everywhere. It was a measure of her peace of mind that she didn't immediately feel threatened by the long shadows and whispering trees.

There were a few people in the water but the wooded paths seemed deserted. She carefully made her way through the trees to the small clearing she and Ruri had picked out. Setting down the bag, she pulled out the lamp she had brought with her and inspected the area. It didn't seem to have been disturbed since the last time they had been there. After setting down the lamp, she reopened the bag and began to set out the items they would be using.

The crunch of a dead leaf made her look up.

Ruri stepped out of the shadows and stopped. She looked around the clearing dispassionately before her gaze came to rest on Thea again. Thea watched as Ruri's gaze chilled.

Oh great, she thought to herself, *here we go again*. That particular look generally preceded a nasty rant on Ruri's part. Thea wasn't really in the mood for it.

"Well, considering how you rolled over for those two freaks you married, I suppose it's no big surprise that you like to munch carpet as well."

Thea's mouth dropped open.

Ruri smirked at her, a hard cold glint in her eyes.

Thea's mouth closed with a snap and her own eyes narrowed. "I so did not hear you just say that," she growled.

"I think you did," was the sneered reply.

Thea simmered. "Just what is your problem?"

Ruri's body fairly vibrated with anger. "My *problem* is that you just go along with everything that has happened! You don't seem to care that you were abducted. That you have no choice about your life. You fawn over those two perverts you live with and *now* you decide to let them marry another woman. Have you no pride? Or a spine?" she spat out venomously.

Thea felt blood rush hotly to her face. "You --"

Ruri cut her off. "Have you ever thought about saying no? Just telling them both to go to hell? *Of course not.* Because that would require you to have some willpower. You make me sick!" she shouted.

Thea had had enough. "How dare you," she snarled, advancing on the other woman. "You bitter, self-absorbed, venomous, hateful *bitch.*" She poked a finger into Ruri's chest. "Let's talk about you for a minute, you evil-tongued hag. You seem to think that everyone has to be like you. Perpetually pissed off! The only time I've *ever* seen you smile was at someone else's misfortune."

Ruri fell back a step, looking startled.

Thea advanced until their noses almost touched. "As for my *husbands*, you will *never* refer to them as 'perverts' again. Do I make myself clear? Nor will you make disparaging remarks about the woman who will soon be my *wife*! I happen to love all of them. And I do *not* answer to you!" Thea poked her in the chest again. "Now, let's talk about our religion. Remember the rule? 'An' it harm none do what thou will'? Or is that only when it's convenient? Are you a wannabe witch? Because that's sure as hell what you are acting like!"

Ruri gasped. "How dare you!"

Thea glared. "I dare much when it comes to my family. You don't even try to get along with them, and if you did you would find out that they are wonderful men. Sya'tia is my best friend and *I* asked her to marry us, not my husbands.

As for 'munching carpet,' as you so quaintly put it, it's none of your fucking business!" Thea panted after she finished yelling that. Her whole body felt tense. She had thought she had left most of this prejudice bullshit behind her on Earth. She knew it had been a vain wish, but she had hoped.

Ruri stared at her in shock for a moment, but Thea could almost see her regroup and puff up with outrage.

"It's none of my business?" Ruri snarled angrily. "So I'm just supposed to sit back and let you make a fool of yourself? Pretend that everything is okay? Next you're going to tell me I should just roll over *like you did* and make pretty with Kiger? Should I pick out a couple of those desperate bitches who can't have kids and marry them too? Because it's always been my life's goal to be a broodmare!"

Thea rolled her eyes. "Okay, drama queen, let's go with that. Maybe if you talked to Kiger instead of *beating him up every time he looks at you wrong* you might find a man you liked! But nooo, you have to abuse him. These people are not like us. They don't think like us. *And* maybe if you *got laid*, you wouldn't be so fucking nasty to everyone!"

Ruri hauled back and slapped Thea across her face.

Thea cried out and stumbled back, cupping her cheek. They stared at each other in shock.

"Okay, that's about enough of that shit." A new voice echoed in the silence that filled the glen.

They both turned and stared at the two women who were entering the warm circle of light cast by the lamp. Two large cats darted in and out of their feet. One had long black fur and the other was a deep orange.

Thea pressed her hand against her stinging face. She watched, bewildered, as both women came to a stop in front of them.

The taller of the two had shoulder-length, curly auburn hair. She was built like an Amazon, with the heavy muscles of a female body builder. Deep blue eyes watched her and Ruri from a strong, square-jawed face. "You slap her again and I'll return the favor for her, little girl." She took Thea's hand away from her face with gentle hands and inspected the skin. "You might bruise and it'll swell for a bit. Put some ice on it when you get home and expect those overprotective men of yours to be all over you about how it happened." She winked at Thea. "I'm Cristabel, by the way. This is Zinnia, my girlfriend." Her head twitched toward the shorter woman standing quietly beside her.

Thea turned her attention to Zinnia. She was a slender blonde with short feathery hair and light brown eyes. Thea smiled tentatively. "Hello."

Zinnia nodded in return before turning her gaze to Ruri. "Well, that was an interesting catfight to listen in on." She leaned against Cristabel. "I especially liked the 'carpet munching' references. It's always nice to know how someone feels about lesbians before you tell them you are one."

Ruri flushed.

Cristabel slung an arm across her girlfriend's shoulders. "We got woken up by two very upset cats. They led us here." She barely spared Ruri a glance. "We know who you are, Thea. The whole ship's been buzzing about you. We found out you were a witch when someone mentioned your necklace, so we had planned on introducing ourselves. We just didn't think it would be like this."

Thea blushed faintly; she knew why they had heard of her. "It's nice to meet you," she mumbled. Not wanting to meet their eyes, she looked around for the cats, but they had disappeared. *Drat!* She had been hoping to see them again. She had her suspicions, not that she was sharing them with her husbands.

Zinnia peered at Ruri. "I think you need to spend some time reading the basic tenets of witchcraft again. You don't seem to understand them very well. The backlash on that slap is gonna be fun. Karma ain't no one's friend. So, is Thea right? Are you a wannabe witch? Someone who does it for shock value instead of a true faith?" She said this with all the calm of a lady asking for a fresh cup of tea. As if the answer didn't matter in the least to her.

Thea believed it was Zinnia's tone more than her words that brought a deep flush of color to Ruri's face. No one liked having their faults pointed out to them, and Zinnia had phrased it in such a way that Thea felt she hadn't expected any better from Ruri. That had to pinch, and Thea wondered what was being said about Ruri to give her that reputation.

Thea could almost see Ruri gathering the tattered cloak of her dignity around her.

Ruri stared down her nose at the newcomers. A remarkable feat since both women were considerably taller than she. "What business is it of yours?"

Cristabel shrugged. "Well, since we were going to ask Thea to form a coven with us, and it seems you're probably going to come along for the ride whether we like it or not, we should know if you're a poser or the real deal."

Ruri grumbled something under her breath in Japanese. Thea didn't bother asking for a translation since the tone conveyed the meaning so well. She sat down on a boulder and watched the byplay. This could get interesting. She already knew the outcome; her Lady had already told her to find her sisters. That thought made her pause for a moment and gave her an idea on how she could smooth things.

"Ladies, please sit down so we can talk comfortably," she said in a quiet voice. The other three women broke off staring each other down and looked at her as if they had forgotten her presence.

Ruri flounced over and threw herself on the ground beside her, and the other two chose to sit facing them.

Thea touched Ruri's shoulder. "I'm sorry for the things I said. I had no right to say them."

Ruri looked up at her in surprise. "I started it. I was so angry when Kiger came home all excited that Sya'tia was wearing a veil. I just don't understand how you can accept them."

Thea decided that was probably as close as she was going to get to an apology. She turned to the two newcomers. "It's nice to meet both of you and we would welcome more sisters. Ruri has a bit of a temper and it sparked mine. But what siblings don't fight occasionally?" She winked at them.

Cristabel grinned, but Zinnia still had a reserved look on her face. Thea wondered if she always looked that remote.

She turned back to Ruri. "I accept them because I spent time getting to know them. They aren't so bad. You have to remember they don't have the same morals and values we do. They evolved their own culture; how can we expect them to be like us? You have to make allowances for that, Ruri, or you'll never be happy." She shrugged. "I liked them and after awhile I loved them." She slid off the rock and leaned back against it.

"Who did you get stuck with, Cristabel? Zinnia?" Thea asked.

Cristabel grinned ruefully. "Shage. He decided that since Zinnia and I were together, he'd get a twofer deal."

Ruri blinked. "Twofer?"

Zinnia sighed. "A two for one deal. Since we were already together, he thought he'd get two wives instead of one. We make him sleep in the spare bedroom."

Thea laughed. "Nice. There's another interesting bit of culture. Since the Ta'e'sha are bisexual they don't understand homosexuality or heterosexuality. Bet he got a shock when the two of you woke up!"

Zinnia stared at Ruri again. "At least we don't beat him up."

Thea winced. This might be more difficult than she had thought.

Zinnia continued, "I know Kiger, he's a pretty nice guy and treats everyone else well. Now I know where the bruises and broken bones are coming from." Her face was very still as she watched Ruri. "My father beat my mother whenever the mood struck him. I don't think a husband beater is any better."

"I am not a husband beater!" Ruri looked outraged.

Thea and Cristabel remained silent.

"And my father firmly believed he wasn't a wife beater. So, what's your excuse? Kiger needed to be 'disciplined'?" Zinnia said, a little more heat in her voice.

"He wouldn't quit touching me!" Ruri shouted. "Every night he crawled into bed with me after I fell asleep! Everywhere I went, there he was! He wouldn't leave me alone! Not even in the bathroom!" All of this burst from her like an infection that had gone too long without being cleaned.

Thea put her hand on Ruri's shoulder. "It has to stop, Ruri. You can't keep up like this. If it continues, Security will get involved whether Kiger wants them to or not. You know that."

Ruri rested her head against Thea's shoulder. "I know. But I don't know what to do. I'm so sick of him stalking me. The only time I feel safe is when I'm at work because Daeshen refuses to allow anyone in who's not on the team…and when I'm with you."

Zinnia's features relaxed marginally. "I'm sure we can think of something if we put our heads together. But stop hurting him."

Cristabel nodded decisively. "Yup. We'll think of something and if that doesn't work… Well, leave him."

Ruri blinked at that, as if the thought had never occurred to her.

Thea nodded. "Yup, you can come stay with us. As long as you lose the 'tude. My guys don't deserve it."

"I know," Ruri said softly.

They all jumped when a black clad figure materialized out of the shadows.

Sya'tia stared at Ruri with icy black eyes. "Do not *ever* strike her again." Her wrist spines sheathed themselves with a soft hiss. "Your manner shames your people, your mate, and your Gods. My husbands-to-be have attempted to be your friends and have swallowed your scorn. I have accepted your barely hidden sneers because Thea counts you as a sister. But know that I will not tolerate her being abused. She has suffered enough." She turned and faded back into the shadows without another word.

Thea jumped to her feet to follow Sya'tia. She had to smother a chuckle when Cristabel's voice rang out behind her. "Wow, Ruri. You have an amazing talent for pissing people off. Have you thought about going into politics?"

* * *

Sya'tia listened to her betrothed crash through the bushes as she tried to catch up.

"Sya? Please wait."

She stopped and turned. Her gaze slid over the mark on Thea's cheek. It glowed with color to her heat sensitive eyes. She suppressed the urge to go back and beat some sense into Ruri's stubborn skull.

"How did you know?" Thea asked her softly.

Sya'tia looked away. She couldn't meet Thea's eyes as she made her confession. "I knew something had hurt you, and when I checked, you weren't in your cabin so I came looking. I felt her striking you, just as I felt it when Barik took you. I didn't know what it was then so I did nothing. If I had paid more attention perhaps you would not have suffered so." Her hair fell forward to hide her face. She didn't want Thea to look at her. "Maybe you wouldn't have lost your child."

Thea's palm cupped her cheek. She looked back at her love sadly.

Thea sighed softly and caressed her cheek. Her eyes were dark with grief. "Sya'tia, you can't live your life on 'maybe' or 'if I had.' It happened, and it wasn't your fault. None of it was your fault. Kyrin and Daeshen were so sick they had to be sedated. Do you blame them?"

Sya'tia shook her head, looking back at the ground again.

"Then how can you blame yourself?"

She shook her head. "I don't know. I just should have done more." Thea's fingers tunneled through her hair and tugged her head up again.

Thea smiled gently. "Silly woman, you're not a Goddess." She stood on tiptoe and kissed her nose. "Let's go cuddle with our men."

Sya'tia grinned. "Just cuddle?"

Thea giggled softly. "We may be able to talk them into something else…"

Chapter Nine

Thea peered around curiously as she cautiously took the last step off the *Dark Queen* and placed her foot on the soil of another planet for the first time. The port was clean, but dusty, and people milled about like ants. Everyone seemed to be in a hurry. Huge ships filled the area in neat rows. Each was as big as a small town. A bright yellow sun glared warmly in a deep cerulean sky.

The breeze carried the scent of the sea and she inhaled deeply. After months of being cooped up on the ship, it was a relief to be under the open sky and breathe air that hadn't been recycled. She turned to look back up at the *Dark Queen*. It was an awe-inspiring sight. She sat like the queen she was named for as maintenance crews swarmed over the outside like cleaner birds on a hippopotamus.

Thea took Kyrin's hand and smiled nervously up at him. He had told her they would be docked for several months while the ship was cleaned and maintained before their next launch. They would be staying with Kyrin's family since he and Daeshen didn't keep a house planet-side.

The trial would be held in the capital city because of Barik's rank. While they were there, they would stay with Daeshen's family. She was feeling very apprehensive about meeting her new in-laws. Hopefully, they would like her.

Sya'tia stepped up beside her and took a deep breath. Kyrin released Thea's hand as she turned to smile up at the taller woman. "Happy to be home?" she asked quietly.

Sya'tia nodded, looking around the dusty docking bays with a contented expression on her face. "Yes, I am. If we have time, I'd like to have the three of you come home with me to meet my family. But it's planting season, so we should probably plan on doing it after the trial. That way we won't be in the way."

"What does your family farm?" Thea asked absently as she watched Kyrin being greeted enthusiastically by a large group of people.

"Sea ferns," Sya'tia replied. "It's a staple for us much like your wheat is. My family has held their land for over seven hundred years," she added proudly.

Thea jumped as Daeshen popped up behind them and threw an arm around each of them.

"What are you two doing standing here? Don't you want to meet Kyrin's family?" he inquired brightly.

Thea gulped as he started towing them toward Kyrin. She started tugging at her skirt and self-consciously straightening her blouse.

The group's chattering died down as they reached them.

Thea shifted from foot to foot as several pairs of eyes studied her and Sya'tia curiously. She darted a pleading look at Kyrin who winked and pulled the tall woman standing beside him forward. It was very obvious she was related to him by her amber hair and dark skin.

She had a broad face with tiny lines around her mouth and eyes as if she smiled often. Her dress was loose and flowing, a pale yellow-green that complemented her coloring.

"Mother, I wish to introduce my mates and betrothed to you. You know Daeshen, who has consented to join my house as husband." He took Thea's hand and placed it in his mother's hand. "This is Theadora Auralel, our first wife." Next he took Sya'tia's hand and placed it over Thea's. "And this is Sya'tia Osan, our betrothed."

Kyrin's mother stared at them impassively for a moment and Thea felt her heart sink. Suddenly she smiled widely. "I am Vashka and welcome you to the House of Auralel." She hugged both Thea and Sya'tia hard and placed gentle kisses on their cheeks before turning to beam at Kyrin. "Not only do you bring me two daughters, but both Chosen! Well done, my son, in catching two such beautiful ladies!" She turned back to Thea and said, "I have borne no daughters and am deeply honored that you took my family name to carry on our line."

Thea smiled in return before slanting a look and raised eyebrow at Kyrin, who flushed faintly. "It is an honor to accept your name and I thank you for your gracious welcome." She wasn't sure what else to say, so she shut up.

Vashka laughed happily before turning to Sya'tia to exclaim over her marriage veil. "Oh, how beautiful! May I touch it? I have never seen such cloth!"

Sya'tia, beaming over the warm welcome, hurried to untie the veil and show it to Vashka. Both women's heads bent together as they inspected the cloth. Two of the men who had greeted Kyrin drifted closer so they could look as well.

Kyrin pulled Thea over to meet a small, delicately boned male with translucent sea green hair and pale green skin. "Darling, I would like you to meet my father, Tosaa. Normally, Mother would introduce you, but I think it will be a bit before she remembers to."

Tosaa took Thea's hands in his and pressed a kiss to her lips. "Welcome, wife of my son. Our family rejoices in your presence in our lives."

Thea smiled shyly and murmured a soft thank you. She leaned against Kyrin, who curled an arm around her waist. The men talked quietly, exchanging news. She watched Daeshen cuddle closer to Sya'tia and point out another detail in the veil. It was a relief to find Kyrin's parents so accepting. It wouldn't be hard to think of his parents as hers. And it would be nice to be part of a family again.

Watching Vashka made her realize just how much she had missed her own mother. Maybe that void would be filled a little now.

Someone tugged on her hair and she turned. A young man, the spitting image of Tosaa, smiled shyly at her from under the heaviest set of lashes Thea had ever seen on a man. His hair was much shorter than she was used to seeing on a Ta'e'shian. It barely brushed his shoulders. "Hello, Theadora," he mumbled.

"Hello. Are you Kyrin's brother?" she asked gently.

He nodded, still peeking up at her shyly through his lashes. "I'm Craedor."

Thea offered her arm to give him the traditional Ta'e'shian greeting. His face lit up and he ran his hand from her elbow to her fingertips. The greeting was usually only used when adults greeted each other, but Thea had always treated kids as adults and had no intention of changing that now.

He sidled closer to her. "I'm twelve and I'm going to be a captain like Kyrin!" he announced.

She grinned. "I see. I'm sure you'll be a very good captain."

He beamed at her and began talking a mile a minute about his career plans, his pet octopus, and something called corgans. As near as she could tell, it was a motor that helped propel the Ta'e'sha through water at great speed.

She noticed that Vashka kept glancing around and targeting Craedor for a moment before returning her attention to the conversation going on around her. Thea suspected that the talkative young man beside her had a tendency to disappear on his mother.

Suddenly his chatter trailed off, bringing Thea's wandering attention back to him. Sya'tia had walked up to them and Craedor was staring up at her in awe. She grinned inwardly. "Craedor, have you met Sya'tia?" she asked gently.

He gulped and shook his head, still staring.

"Sya, this is Craedor, our little brother," she said.

Sya'tia nodded gravely. "Greetings, little brother. You favor your father." She offered him her arm.

Craedor smiled shyly as he caressed her arm. He shifted from foot to foot for a moment. "Can I see your fangs?" he finally blurted out in a rush.

Sya'tia laughed softly and winked at Thea before opening her mouth and slowly extending her fangs. They gleamed in the sunlight for a moment before she retracted them again.

He stared at her in awe.

"You look funny," he stated after a moment.

Sya'tia's face fell.

"Kinda like the Goddess, Shaysha," he mumbled shyly, not noticing how Sya'tia had started to draw back. "She's my favorite because she's the prettiest. But don't tell the other Goddesses I said that," he added hastily. "They are pretty too."

His face took on a crafty gleam. "If you wait a few years you could marry me instead." He blinked flirtatiously up at her from under his lashes. "I'll be even handsomer than Kyrin. Promise. And you'd be first wife." He ended his proposal with a sly smile.

Sya'tia laughed with delight and hugged him tightly. "Such a tempting offer, my handsome one, but then I wouldn't have my beloved Thea and I don't think we could pry her away from your brother."

He sighed theatrically. "I guess."

Craedor immediately launched into another round of excited questioning, reminding Thea of Kati. As Sya'tia patiently answered him, Thea wondered where her pink-haired friend was. She hadn't seen her for several days; the rush to prepare for going planet-side had taken over everyone's lives.

Minutes later, they were all being bundled into a craft that hovered above the ground before speeding off. Craedor wiggled between Thea and a Sya'tia, still chattering happily. They landed half an hour later at a large house on the outskirts of the city. Thea was slightly disappointed they didn't have time to stop and look around, but Kyrin had assured her they would visit the city later.

Vashka showed them into a suite that had a separate bathing area and a huge bed. The room was decorated in shades of rose-gold and tan. She hugged each of them again. "I'll have your luggage sent up directly. Dinner isn't for several hours, so please relax and unpack. Kyrin knows where everything is." She beamed happily at them for a moment before leaving.

Thea explored the room curiously while Sya'tia flopped down on the bed tiredly. There was a large glass tub set in one corner. It was filled with pale blue water and had a large curved lip along one side. It reminded her of an old style Victorian bathtub. A case filled with books was set within arm's reach. "What's this?" she asked curiously.

Daeshen came to stand beside her and swirled his hand through the water. "It's a therapeutic reading bath." He sniffed his fingers then offered his hand to Thea.

Thea inhaled lightly. The water had a spicy scent to it. "Wow, are the books waterproof?"

He nodded. "Kyrin was always spraining something so Tosaa finally had one installed in his bedroom. I guess they moved it in here when Kyrin commed them to tell them we were coming."

Thea grinned. "Well, he hasn't changed in that. Which reminds me: we're getting low on his therapy salts." She glanced behind her and saw Kyrin leering at Sya'tia. "Sya'tia's been kicking his bootie at practice."

She jumped when two hands grabbed her butt and squeezed.

"Mmm, bootie," Daeshen breathed into her ear.

Thea turned around and looped her arms around his neck. Her lips feathered lightly across his. "I thought you would be worn out from this morning." She nipped his nose. "You were in rare form."

He smirked down at her. "I'll never be too tired to fulfill my duties, my love."

She shivered as his nimble fingers started inching her skirt up. The proof of his statement was pressing into her stomach.

Daeshen leered. "Wanna play 'tentacles' again?" He succeeded in getting his hands under her skirt and quickly slid them into the panties she still insisted on wearing. He hadn't told her, but he had sent off a com to one of his favorite tailors and asked if several new sets could be made out of lace for both her and Sya'tia. He and Kyrin had high hopes of a fashion show when the order was delivered.

Thea giggled against his throat. "No tentacles, but maybe later."

He grinned and nuzzled her hair. During one of his searches through the movie database, he had run across some animated movies from Japan. Curious, he had pulled one up to watch and nearly had the skin singed off him. He had serious concerns about the minds that had created some of them. They barely scraped erotic and went straight on to creepy. He loved that term. It was one he had picked up from his wife. But he had discovered that Thea liked some "anime," as she called it, and was rather delighted by the "tentacle" possibilities of her husbands' hair.

He slid his hands out of her panties and under her butt and lifted her against his muscular frame. Catching her mouth with his, he walked them toward the bed and fell back onto it with Thea under him. He shivered when she nibbled on his neck. Sliding her panties down her legs he stole a kiss.

Kyrin's weight landing beside them made the mattress bounce lightly under them. He turned his head to watch his husband passionately kiss Sya'tia. He turned his attention back to Thea, who was lazily untying the laces of his shift. Humming softly in his throat he tossed her panties across the room and attacked the buttons down the side of her skirt. It continued to delight him that his little wife enjoyed wearing skirts, because, after all, they were so easy to get her out of.

He rolled her on top of him and pulled the now loosened skirt free. Thea pulled her mouth from his and sat up, straddling his lap. Her hips swayed, grinding against his erection as she wiggled out of her shirt. It joined the rest of her clothing on the floor. His hands slid up her belly to cup the full weight of her breasts. He stroked her velvety nipples, delighted when they immediately hardened to sharp points.

Soft noises beside him made him turn his head. Kyrin was stretched out on Sya'tia. Their mouths fed lazily on each other. It caused the flame in his groin to leap even higher. He loved watching Kyrin make love to Thea and Sya'tia.

He looked back up at Thea who was watching Kyrin and Sya'tia with heavy eyes. She was rocking herself back and forth against the length of his cock. Her hands came up to cup his cock and she purred softly, rolling her head languidly.

He freed his hands and started wiggling out of his clothing, making her giggle softly. He succeeded in getting his shirt off, but had to tickle Thea to get her to move so he could shimmy out of his pants.

Thea slid back onto him and smiled down at him. Her arms stretched out above his head as she lowered her mouth to brush her lips across his lightly. He slid his arms around her and cradled her hips, gently massaging the firm muscles under her silky skin. He and Kyrin had been much gentler with Thea since the attack. They were uneasy about playing their tie-me-up games and risking another black eye or bloody nose. They didn't want to trigger another panic attack. Their dainty wife had a wicked right hook.

A thump beside them made him look over quickly. Kyrin squawked as Sya'tia neatly flipped him onto his belly and pinned him down. Sya'tia leaned down to scrape her fangs across the back of Kyrin's neck. His husband went motionless the moment those pearly white teeth touched him.

Thea cuddled closer and watched as well, her fingers tunneling into Daeshen's hair to massage his scalp. He hummed with pleasure. He loved that; it made shivers break out across his whole body. Her smooth fingers moved in slow circles and her fingernails scratched lightly along the thin muscles of his hair.

Sya'tia pulled Kyrin's shirt down his back, lapping slowly at the exposed honey brown skin. "Think you can take me, big man?" she whispered against his skin.

Kyrin rumbled under her.

Daeshen smirked. Kyrin had tried his dominant games when Sya'tia had first joined their bed. It hadn't turned out quite the way he'd expected. Before he knew it, he had been tied up, on his back, straddled, and "ridden like an unbroken horse" as Thea had stated with awe.

He had found Sya'tia to be an enthusiastic and passionate partner. She melded well into the rhythms of his family and matched Kyrin for aggressiveness and sheer stubbornness. Sometimes it felt as if she had always been part of their family.

He rolled onto his side and guided Thea until her back was against his chest and they could both watch the play between Sya'tia and Kyrin.

Daeshen pulled Thea's leg back over his and slowly pressed the head of his cock into her now wet sheath. He sank easily into her, savoring the slick muscles twitching around him. He stilled and cupped his hand over Thea's hip, holding her motionless. After a moment, she wiggled her hips. His hand tightened, holding her still. Moisture seeped from her, wetting his thigh. He loved how wet she became. He withdrew and thrust hard into her again.

Thea cried out, arching back.

He stilled again.

She writhed against him, trying to tease him into giving her what she wanted. It was a trick of hers he knew well. He reached between her legs and pinched her clit.

Her head pressed back against his shoulder as she moaned throatily. Her wet sex rocked urgently against his fingers. His cock moved slowly in and out of her with each motion. He felt an arm slide around his waist and looked to see Sya'tia press her mouth against Thea's.

Thea's hands came up to cup Sya'tia's face as she returned the deep kiss.

Daeshen began to move faster inside Thea as he watched their tongues twine around each other lazily. All three of them rocked as Kyrin entered Sya'tia from behind and began thrusting inside her urgently.

He bit the back of Thea's neck and moaned, grinding himself in slow circles against her ass. His eyes fluttered closed as Sya'tia's leg slid over his and Thea's and she ground herself against the back of his hand as he continued to toy with Thea's clit. The feel of their smooth, hairless pussies was pure ecstasy. He gripped one of the rings that pierced Thea's lower lips and tugged gently.

He drew almost completely out of her and then thrust back in hard and fast. Her sweet sheath made moist sucking sounds with each thrust and his dainty little wife moaned into Sya'tia's lips.

He opened his eyes and locked gazes with his husband. They shared a look of mutual bliss. Kyrin smiled slowly at him as he worked his cock smoothly in and out of their betrothed. His gaze moved over their women. Sya'tia's pale blue-white skin was pressed firmly against the warmer pink tones of Thea's and set like a pale jewel in the honey brown of Kyrin's. He pulled his hand from between their legs to stroke them both.

Kyrin, his gaze still locked on Daeshen's face, slowly pulled himself from Sya'tia, who moaned in protest. He slowly climbed over both women and curled himself around Daeshen's back. Daeshen groaned softly as Kyrin's cock, still wet with Sya'tia's juices, probed between the cheeks of his ass. It slowly slid within, stretching him almost unbearably.

It had been so long since he had felt Kyrin moving within him.

He sent a brief thought to Sya'tia who was still nibbling on Thea's lips. She responded by moving up along Thea's body and presenting her wet sex to Thea's mouth. The small holes on the lips of her labia looked red and flushed from the tendrils that made up Kyrin's pubic hair looping through them to hold their bodies locked together.

His wife curled her arm around Sya'tia's hip and lapped delicately at the offered flesh.

Daeshen's attention was abruptly drawn back to Kyrin who had just thrust powerfully into him again. He growled against Thea's neck and rolled his hips back into his husband's.

Thea bent away from him slightly as she pleasured Sya'tia. She whined softly each time Daeshen jolted inside her. He gritted his teeth and clutched her hip, holding her steady as Kyrin rocked and jolted them both with his urgent movements.

Sya'tia pulled Daeshen's hair gently and he looked up at her. She smiled and slid a finger into his mouth. He curled his tongue around it and sucked slowly, working her finger like a cock. Her eyes closed and she rocked gently against Thea's working mouth. Daeshen hummed softly as he watched them together. It was a sight he'd never thought he'd be blessed with.

He moaned when Kyrin nudged his knee between Daeshen's legs and rubbed his balls with his thigh. He felt overwhelmed from all the sensations flowing over his skin. It was too much. Abruptly, his frills popped open, and he convulsed against Thea as his cock bathed her insides with his potent seed. He writhed against her ass as Kyrin continued to pound his with punishing strokes. He reveled in the taking even as he understood the ferocity behind it. His darling husband had been gentle too long and just wanted to fuck. Sometimes they just needed to pound themselves without caution until they bubbled over.

He pushed his fingers back between Thea's slick dripping lips and stroked her erect little clit. As his climax waned, he now savored the approaching orgasms of his mates.

Thea was bucking and writhing into his fingers as she made little whimpering noises against Sya'tia's slick pussy. Her own wet channel contracted violently around him and she gave a muffled scream, twitching around him. He continued his tender ministrations, not letting her climax slow but trying to keep it going as long as he could.

After a couple of minutes, she weakened and moaned softly. His frills folded down and his ass burned from Kyrin's slapping plunges.

Thea pulled away from him and panted softly. Sya'tia slid back to give her room; she looked faintly disappointed, Daeshen thought.

Kyrin pulled him hard against him and rolled him onto his belly. Daeshen turned his face to the side as Kyrin hunched over him, still thrusting feverishly. He felt dazed from the force and passion behind that hammering prick.

Thea pushed Sya'tia onto her back and settled herself between her legs again. He smiled as her fingers came up to toy with Sya'tia's erect nipples and her tongue buried itself in the taller woman's tight channel.

Above him, Kyrin grunted and jerked. His frills opened and hot jets of cum sprayed inside Daeshen. His muscular husband curled over Daeshen's back and panted hoarsely. He murmured soft love words and his hands caressed Daeshen's sweaty chest and back. Daeshen smiled lazily, soaking up all of it.

They rolled onto their sides, still attached, and watched Thea and Sya'tia.

Blue-white thighs cupped their wife's cheeks, hiding her face from his view. Thea's dark red black curls were draped across Sya'tia's leg and shimmered softly in the light. Her legs slid under her and her ass arched into the air as her busy mouth continued its task.

Sya'tia threaded her fingers through Thea's hair and her hips jerked and danced. She was humming, low and breathy, in her throat as she quickly approached the edge of her own pleasure.

Daeshen wished he could record this to watch over and over again. He cuddled deeper into Kyrin's embrace as he continued to caress and explore Daeshen's sated body.

Suddenly, Sya'tia roared softly, her body arching into a taut bow. She trembled and jerked, almost knocking Thea off her. Her fangs gleamed from her open mouth. After a timeless moment she relaxed again and took a deep shuddering breath.

He almost laughed when Thea peeked at him from over Sya'tia's thigh. She looked smug. His wife climbed up Sya'tia's body to exchange sated kisses and soft words.

His eyes grew heavy watching them as the events of the day snuck up on him and he let himself drift off to sleep. They had time for a nap before dinner.

* * *

Condezl crouched on the edge of a wall and inspected the workers moving around under him. *"Fresh meat! What shall we do to torment our new prey, my pretties?"*

Myst rustled her feathers. *"Let's steal their tools. I bet we can tie them to the trees. Oh! How about we leave more 'mementos' in their tool boxes?"*

Condezl chuffed happily. *"Sounds good. I'll put the gang on it today."*

Chapter Ten

Thea yawned and looked around sleepily. Sya'tia and her husbands were still asleep. She carefully wiggled her way free of the warm tangle of limbs and stretched. It seemed like she left them sleeping a lot. Rubbing the last remnants of sleep from her eyes, she padded into the bathroom to clean up.

When she was finished, she went back into the bedroom to put on fresh clothing and slipped out of the bedroom. She wandered down the hall, following the tempting aromas issuing from the kitchen.

Vashka looked up when she entered the room. She grinned knowingly and Thea felt heat rush into her cheeks. "Hello, Mother." She stopped, unsure. "May I call you Mother?" she asked hesitantly.

Vashka wiped her hands on a towel before cupping Thea's cheeks in her hands. "I would like nothing better," she said sincerely.

Thea smiled. "Is there anything I can do to help?"

Vashka returned to the counter. "Just sit with me; dinner is all ready but for the cooking. Tell me about your family." She poured two cups of tea from a thermal carafe and sat with Thea at the small table tucked in a corner.

"Well, my family is from a country called Ireland, originally. They moved to the United States of America about one hundred years ago," she began, knowing most of it would be lost on Vashka. "Great-Grandpa was a farmer and Great-Grandma was a weaver."

Vashka nodded, sipping her tea.

"They moved to the state of Oregon and lived in a little town called Eagle Creek." She grinned. "Great-Grandpa started an apple orchard; those are a type of fruit tree."

"They had a daughter and Great-Grandma taught her how to weave. When she got married, her husband, my grandfather, helped with the orchard. He also made furniture. They had one daughter as well, and she became a weaver too. All the women in my family have been weavers as long as anyone can remember." She paused to sip her tea. "Dad didn't know anything about farming; he was a mechanic. So when he married Mom, Grandma and Grandpa sold the farm and moved in with them."

"That's too bad," Vashka said sadly.

"Not really," Thea said with a smile. "Dad had a black thumb; plants didn't respond to him at all. Unfortunately, the people who bought the property cut down the orchard and built houses on the land. That's what's sad. I loved those trees."

Vashka shook her head at the idea. The Ta'e'sha had a great respect for the land and were very careful about where they built their houses. Many of them still lived in the sea, building in the rock cliffs and sandy areas where little grew. On land they placed homes in more barren areas as well, saving the fertile soil for growing.

Thea continued, "We moved to the outskirts of Portland, and Dad opened a mechanic shop with the money and bought a big house. Mom started weaving cloth for the patchouli and granola crowd. The environmentalists," she explained when Vashka looked confused. "Oregon has a lot of them. They are trying to help people live with the land better, recycle, and use organic products instead of stuff that causes pollution."

"Oh, I see." Vashka still looked a little confused, but motioned for Thea to continue.

"Mom and Dad wanted a big family, but Mom had so much trouble carrying me that the doctors told her she shouldn't try to have any more kids. They tried anyway, but Mom had three miscarriages before they gave up." Thea fiddled with her cup. She had been too young to remember the miscarriages, but she had vague memories of her mother crying sometimes.

Vashka frowned. "Your family is not very fertile," she said meditatively.

Thea shrugged. "Not on Mom's side, but Dad's side is. Dad had a big family, but he didn't talk about them. I guess he got into a really hairy fight with his dad when he was younger and he never spoke to him or the rest again. Not too surprising" -- she grinned mischievously -- "Dad's family was Irish too, and the Irish are known for having nasty tempers and holding grudges. Dad said when he got old he'd get Irish Alzheimer's. He'd forget everything but the grudges."

Vashka smiled uncertainly, but Thea could see she didn't get the joke. "Dad's family actually ran to twins," she went on. "Mom taught me weaving, and I helped her and tried to get a clientele of my own started. When I was eighteen,

Mom, Dad, and my grandparents took a vacation to the coast and were killed in a car accident." Thea looked at the tea in her cup, remembering the police coming to her door with the news. A shaft of pain tore at her heart. "A car full of teenagers was driving too fast and swerved into the wrong lane and hit my family's car head-on." Vashka's hand covered hers and she clung to it. "I was supposed to go with them, but I had been sick with food poisoning so I stayed home. A friend and I ate at a restaurant that wasn't very careful about storing food.

"I sold the house -- it was too big and empty for one person -- and the shop. I moved into an apartment and started waiting tables and working on my weaving. And several years later, I met Kyrin and Daeshen." She glossed over that part, thinking that if Vashka knew the truth she'd rip into both men and tear them new ones. Besides who really wanted to tell their new mother-in-law that her son was into B&D? "So, here I am." She smiled.

Vashka squeezed her hand. "Hmmm, that's quite a story." She pinned Thea with a shrewd stare. "And it's obvious you adored your mother and grandmother, so why did you give up their name?"

Thea smiled slowly and threw Kyrin to the wolves without a qualm. "On Earth it is customary for women to take their husband's name." She waited while Vashka digested that.

The older women's eyes narrowed. "And my darling son didn't tell you we do things differently, did he?"

"Nope," Thea stated cheerfully.

Vashka's face fell. "Well, now that you know differently I would understand if you wish to use your family's name," she said sadly.

"No, no," Thea said, quickly, covering the older woman's hand. "I would be honored to take your name." She hadn't meant to hurt her feelings. "I've missed being part of a family and would love to be part of yours," she stated sincerely.

Vashka smiled slowly, her face filling with happiness again. "I would like that. I've always wanted a daughter." She laughed delightedly. "Now I have two!" Her smile suddenly took a decidedly evil turn. "And I'll talk to Kyrin about his little trick. He may be a grown man but I can still turn him over my knee. Bah, tricking his wife like that! I raised him better than that! I'll chew on Daeshen too, for good measure."

Thea grinned. "Can I watch?"

Vashka chuckled. "Indeed you can, my sweet. I'll teach you the finer points of managing men." She wiggled her eyebrows.

Thea giggled. "You only have one husband?" she asked suddenly.

Vashka grinned. "Yes, just Tosaa, and he's a handful. We didn't find anyone else we wanted to ask to join us. Kyrin got his aggressive nature from his father. Something I've always taken great delight in!" Her grin took on a decidedly lecherous cast.

"And I shall be happy to be aggressive for you tonight, my love," Tosaa stated as he entered the kitchen. He bent to press a kiss onto Vashka's brow. He turned to Thea and stroked her cheek tenderly. "How is my new daughter?" he asked with a smile.

"Fine, thank you" -- she leaned into his hand -- "Father." It seemed right to call this man Father. He did remind her of her own father. They had the same quiet strength. They both looked at their wives with the same love.

Tosaa smiled and caressed her hair. He turned back to his wife. "What's for dinner?"

Thea had to grin as Vashka answered him. It seemed that race had nothing to do with men's stomachs. She turned as Sya'tia glided in stifling a yawn. "Hey, sweetie. Have a nice nap?"

Sya'tia nodded sleepily and collapsed in the chair next to her. "Kyrin will be down in a bit. He's been getting calls from the maintenance crews." She slid Thea a sideways look. "From what he told me, tools are disappearing."

Thea smiled serenely. "They'll turn up." Her mates had been trying to pry information out of her since the asana had returned from their meditations. The messages they had received from their Gods told them the Ta'e'sha had torked off some of the human women's deities and that they would have to find a solution to the problem themselves.

As a result, Kyrin had been hounding Thea for "rituals of appeasement." Thea had stood firm that no ritual would work unless the heart was behind it since the heart was what meant the most in any ritual. Not that she knew any such "ritual."

Plus, she didn't know much more than they did. Sure, she had her suspicions, but that wasn't the same as knowing. So, why should she make comments that might prove to be wrong?

Her attention was brought back to the present by Vashka asking her and Sya'tia to set the table in the dining room. She gathered up the dishes handed to her and followed the older woman, humming softly under her breath.

* * *

They spent several weeks with Kyrin's family. Thea and Sya'tia thrived on the instant acceptance they found in Vashka's home. Kyrin's father took them on tours of the city and helped Thea fine-tune her understanding of the Ta'e'shian written language.

Craedor was an almost constant companion. He dragged Thea and Sya'tia to his school to introduce them to his teachers. They *had* to meet all of his friends and he taught them how to play several games.

Kyrin teased his little brother often about how he dominated their attention. He told Craedor he was in danger of having his wives stolen away from him.

Craedor just grinned and continued to soak up the attention.

Kyrin's other brothers lived outside of town and Thea didn't get to spend as much time with them. They all seemed nice and genuinely glad to have Thea and Sya'tia in their family, but they were busy with their own lives. None of them were married, which Thea found strange, but she didn't ask them about it. It didn't seem polite.

A date for the trial was set and they were quickly approaching the day they would have to leave for Daeshen's home. He became very quiet a few days before they left and barely spoke a word. Thea tried to ask him what was wrong but he wouldn't answer her. She knew he had been getting messages from home and he seemed more withdrawn with each one he received.

She caught Kyrin in a hall the day they were packing to leave.

"What's going on with Daeshen?" she asked quietly, holding Kyrin's sleeve.

Kyrin shook his head. "I don't know. He won't tell me either."

Thea sighed. "Well, he's going to have to talk to us sooner or later. Or I'll have Sya'tia tie him up until he tells us."

Kyrin smiled wanly. Daeshen's attitude had begun to affect them all. There was a tension that hadn't been present before.

Thea walked with him to their bedroom to get the last of the cases. They had hired a driver to take them to Daeshen's family's home.

During the trip she tried to keep conversation going, but everyone was acutely aware of Daeshen's silence as he stared out the window at the passing scenery.

She tried to touch his emotions to see if she could discern what was bothering him but he had his mental walls slammed shut and triple locked. Finally, she reached over and pinched his chin, turning his face to hers. He tried to pull away, but she increased the pressure of her fingers until he met her eyes.

Thea was aware of the other occupants of the vehicle stilling and falling silent. She ignored it. "You and I are going to have a talk tonight. You are not going to argue with me. Is that clear?" she said, her gaze locked firmly with his.

He nodded, his beautiful blue eyes dark with misery.

A few minutes later they arrive at the gates of a grand-looking estate. The house was huge and the lawn perfectly landscaped and maintained. "Wow," Thea breathed, "you grew up here?"

Daeshen shrugged. "We moved here when I was fourteen." He glanced at Kyrin. "I didn't want to. I wanted to stay closer to Kyrin."

Thea pulled her gaze away from the house to look at her husband. "You've known each other that long?"

Kyrin nodded, curling an arm around her shoulders. "Yup, since we could walk almost. Our mothers used to take us to the same park."

"Cool."

They stopped in front of the house and piled out of the vehicle, stretching. The drive had taken several hours and they were all stiff and ready to move around again. The driver began taking their belongings out of the trunk.

Daeshen trudged up the steps and rang the bell.

It was opened several moments later by a tall, dignified man. "Welcome home, Master Daeshen. Your mother is waiting for you in the library. Your father and second mother are away on business and will not return until the week after next."

Daeshen nodded. "Thank you, Sheen." He seemed to brace himself before entering. "This way. I'll introduce you to my mother."

They followed him into the huge foyer. Thea and Sya'tia looked around curiously.

He paused at a door and knocked before opening it. An older woman sat at a large desk with ornate carvings. Her topaz blue hair was pulled back from her face in a braided twist.

Daeshen closed the door after they entered and the woman looked up.

Her deep blue eyes were the exact shade of Daeshen's, only much colder. Her face formed into tight lines as she examined them all slowly. She didn't seem pleased by what she saw.

She stood and held a hand out to her son.

Daeshen crossed the room to grasp it. He turned and motioned for them to come closer. "Mother, you are looking well," he said formally. "May I present my wife, Theadora, my husband, Kyrin, and our betrothed, Sya'tia? Ladies, please meet my mother, Chisha Shoarya."

Chisha pulled her hand free. "This is what you bring me?" she asked coldly. "A deformed commoner and a *thing*?"

Thea sucked in a sharp breath. She heard Sya'tia choke back a cry of pain and steeled her face to not let the hurt and anger show. Kyrin growled softly and crowded closer to her and Sya'tia.

"Mother!" Daeshen blurted out, his voice shocked.

Chisha turned to glare at her son. "I always knew you would take Kyrin. Fine, but you had several opportunities to marry into a *pure* household. A *royal* house. Instead, you bring me this!" She waved her hand vaguely in Thea's direction. "What will my grandchildren look like? Half-breed mongrels at best, deformed monsters at worst! You shame your blood!"

Sya'tia sucked in a sobbing breath, staring at Daeshen as if he had stabbed her in the heart. She turned away to bury her face in Kyrin's shoulder.

Thea pulled away from Kyrin and moved to stand in front of Daeshen, facing Chisha. "How dare you? I will not tolerate you speaking to my husband like that! And if you say one more word about Sya'tia I will feed it to you!" She'd be damned before she let someone treat her family like that and not say a word.

Chisha's head jerked; she obviously hadn't expected anyone to confront her.

Thea turned to Daeshen. "We are so going to talk about this later!" she hissed in English.

"So as well as being ugly you have no manners!" Chisha sneered.

She turned back to Chisha. "I have no manners? You have no room to talk! This introduction is over. Don't bother talking to me or Sya'tia again unless you have something to say that won't get you hit in the face." Thea turned on her heel and marched for the door, ignoring the outraged gasp behind her. "Daeshen. Bedroom. Now," she snarled.

She opened the door, but turned when she didn't hear any footsteps behind her. Everyone was staring at her like she had grown a second, and very ugly, head. "NOW!" she barked.

They all jumped and her mates hurried to her side.

"Daeshen, get back here!" Chisha ordered.

Thea stared hard at the older woman. "Shut that bear trap you call a mouth. He may be your son, but he's my husband, and I'll be damned if I'm leaving him here for you to shred." She yanked Daeshen out the door. Kyrin and Sya'tia quickly followed. She considered slamming the door, but restrained herself. Her mother raised a lady.

Daeshen hung his head, looking even more miserable if that was possible. Thea searched Kyrin's face. He was staring at her in amazement. Sya'tia looked crushed, her beautiful black eyes filled with tears.

"I always forget about your temper, my love," Kyrin said in a wondering voice. "I don't think anyone has ever done that to Chisha before."

Thea glowered. "What, no one has ever had the balls to tell her she's a bitch?" She stood in front of Daeshen and grabbed his ears pulling his face down to hers. "I want to talk to you privately. Right now."

He nodded as best he could, considering she wouldn't let go of his ears. "Sheen, could you show us up to our suite, please?" he asked without turning.

"Of course, Master Daeshen. Your belongings have already been taken up. If you will follow me?" Face impassive, the butler turned and walked away.

"Thea…" Daeshen began, in a pleading voice.

Thea's hand flew up in a halt gesture as she followed Sheen. She wasn't in the mood to listen to his excuses just then. Kyrin put his hand over Daeshen's mouth and shook his head warningly.

Thea ignored the byplay and tried to calm herself.

Sheen paused at a door and opened it. "Will this suit?" he asked Thea.

Thea glanced inside. "It's fine, thank you, Mister Sheen."

Sheen nodded, his face warming a bit. "You are welcome, Mistress. Please call if you need assistance." He closed the door after they entered the room.

Thea took a deep calming breath and looked around, giving herself a few moments. In disbelief, she took in the room. It was all white. Every stick of furniture, every scrap of fabric. White. It was the future poster child for stain removing detergent. Thea wondered what idiot would decorate an entire room in unrelieved white.

Finally, she turned and looked at Sya'tia. She took the taller woman's face in her hands. "Don't listen, love. She doesn't matter. We love you, we want you, and I think you are the most beautiful woman I have ever seen. I feel privileged you are willing to share your life and children with me."

Sya'tia gave her a wobbly smile. "I know. It just surprised me."

Next, she turned to Daeshen. "Your mother is a nasty-tempered bitch, and I really want to know why you didn't feel it was necessary to warn Sya'tia and me of that little fact. And don't try to tell me you had no idea she would react this way because I'm not buying."

He stared at the floor like it was the most fascinating thing he had ever seen. "I was hoping if I gave her some time she'd get used to the idea."

"Uh-huh. Didn't work, did it?"

He shook his head, not looking at her.

"Daeshen, look at me," she said quietly.

He slowly met her eyes.

"You need to tell us when something is bothering you. We can't help if we don't know. I can ignore your mother if I have to, but we live with you. We are here to support you, but we can't do that if you don't communicate." She caressed his cheek, moving to press her body against his. "I won't pretend I'm happy right now, but I'm not angry with you. Well," she hedged, "not too angry."

He smiled wanly. "I'm sorry." He turned to look at Kyrin and Sya'tia. "I am so sorry. I was hoping it wouldn't be like this. You were all so happy with Kyrin's family. I wanted you to be happy with mine too."

Sya'tia curled her arm around his waist and kissed his cheek. "It's not your fault, Daeshen. You are not responsible for her actions."

Thea curled her arms around both of them. She tensed as a thought struck her. "Is your whole family going to be like this?" she asked nervously.

He shook his head. "I don't think Dad and Larasin will be mean. Dad seemed happy for me when I sent messages. Larasin is Dad's second wife. She's really nice."

Thea looked up. "Dad's second wife?" she asked carefully. "Not your parents' second wife?"

"No. Mother accepted Larasin as wife under duress and has never treated her fairly..." His voice trailed off.

"I thought everyone in the marriage had to agree." Thea didn't like all of these surprises.

"Mother had to agree because Dad said he would leave her if she didn't."

Thea winced. The Ta'e'sha didn't have anything like divorce, so, for his father to leave would have been a huge blow to the reputations of both families. "Why did they get married if they couldn't live together?" It was very normal for engaged couples to live together for at least a year before the marriage took place to be sure they were compatible. They hadn't decided on a date for the wedding to Sya'tia yet, but Thea didn't think it would take a full year for them to decide.

Daeshen looked anywhere but at her. "The marriage was arranged by their parents."

Thea sighed gustily. "This is like a regency romance novel!"

Kyrin stirred from where he was leaning against a bedpost. "Leave it, Thea. There's nothing to be done for it. Chisha is a pain, but you can handle her. You've already proved that." He turned to the pile of suitcases. "Let's get unpacked. I imagine that dinner will be soon and probably formal."

Thea had her reservations about unpacking, but followed Kyrin's lead. She kissed Daeshen slowly and nibbled on his lips for a moment. "I love you."

He smiled slowly, his eyes finally starting to lighten and stole another kiss before turning to Sya'tia to do the same.

Chapter Eleven

Thea looked up from her embroidery when Sya'tia slammed the door shut. Both women spent most of their time in the bedroom. Hiding from Chisha. The woman seemed to be physically unable to see one of them without making a nasty comment or harassing them.

"I hate her!" Sya'tia stated in a low, passionate voice. She spun around and paced in front of Thea. "That woman has the mouth of a *meecha*!"

Thea calmly set her hoop aside and folded her hands in her lap. "She is, indeed, a skanky bitch."

Sya'tia gave her a startled look. She stopped pacing and started to grin. "Skanky bitch?"

Thea smiled demurely. "Would you prefer heinous whore? Vile harpy? Or, perhaps, Ruri's evil twin?"

Sya'tia giggled.

Thea had given up all but the barest pretense of courtesy the second day after they had arrived. About the time Chisha had commented she should have taken some training before selling her body. She knew Chisha had found out Thea's culture wasn't very accepting of prostitution and was using it as yet another barb.

A soft knock at the door stopped Thea from continuing.

Sya'tia answered it. A petite, young Ta'e'shian girl stood in the hallway. She looked like a miniature version of Chisha. Her hair had pulled itself back in a tight knot and she wore a gray gown with a pale brown plant motif.

She held out her hands formally. "I am Fwa'twee, Daeshen's sister, I have come to welcome my new sisters." She looked nervous. "I have been staying with friends and only just returned."

Sya'tia smiled and drew her into the room and closed the door. She stroked the girl's hands. "I am Sya'tia, betrothed of the family Auralel."

Thea stood and hugged the girl, ignoring the way she stiffened slightly. "I am Thea, Daeshen's wife. It's a pleasure to meet you, Fwa'twee; I've always wanted a sister."

The girl smiled shyly. "My brothers call me Tweet."

"Oh, that's cute! I like it. Would you like to sit with us?" Thea motioned toward the chairs she had dragged into a circle so her family could chat comfortably. She sat down after the others had taken seats.

"So, Tweet, tell us about yourself." She picked up her embroidery hoop again.

Tweet settled gingerly into the chair. She surreptitiously studied the women her oldest brother had chosen. Sya'tia seemed very stern and forbidding to her with her hunter black eyes and strange features. She had a long oval face, but it looked like the Gods had smoothed her features back with sure strokes leaving them looking subtly elongated. Her eyes were pointed along the outer edge and tilted up exotically. The pure black of her hunter lens made Tweet feel twitchy and nervous. She didn't understand why the woman had left them exposed. There was no danger in Tweet's home. High cheekbones slashed upward and carried the barest hint of lavender in her icy blue skin.

That combined with her thicker than normal hair finally made her realize why the woman looked so odd to her. *Birth defects*, she decided. She looked like she should have been born a few thousand years ago. There were pictures of their people's ancestors who looked like Sya'tia. Thick bands of black in the hair around her temples stood out in stark contrast against the snowy white color of the rest, marking her as a Warrior Chosen.

She felt a sudden surge of sympathy for the woman. Chisha was probably rabid that Daeshen was going to marry an imperfect woman. And too, his first wife was a human. This told her why her mother had wanted her to stay away. Chisha wouldn't want her daughter being "tainted."

She turned her attention to her new sister, who was serenely doing needlepoint.

Thea looked soft, mothering, and very exotic. Tweet was startled to see Thea carried not one set of God-marks, but all sets. Who was this tiny woman who drew so much attention from Tweet's Gods? White filigree laced along Thea's cheekbones and shimmered gently when the woman moved her head. There was a stylized gray setting sunburst on her forehead, just above the center of her eyebrows. Aquamarine leaves and starbursts twined around her wrists and the back of her hands and disappeared into her sleeves. Red flames traced along her collarbones where Thea had left the top of her blouse open.

Tweet had to stare to see the black markings in Thea's near black hair. She wouldn't have noticed them except that unlike other Warrior Chosen they weren't mere bands of black but heavy locks that absorbed light.

She felt very intimidated by both women and had no idea how she would be able to interact with them. Or, if they would even want her around.

She had seen a few human women and they all looked so very different from each other. Why, one woman had skin that was almost black! None of her people were so dark! She had reminded Tweet of the statues of Kashka, the Dark Goddess of war. Her children would be beautiful if they took after their mother.

She peeked at Thea once again.

Her mother had contacted her and told her to stay with her friend until Daeshen's family left. That had made her curious and she decided to come home and see what had her mother so upset. Now she knew. Her mother was obsessed with their family being distantly related to a royal clan. She had been trying to force Daeshen into an advantageous marriage since before Tweet was born. She had a feeling the pressure would be transferred to her now.

She didn't understand it at all. Her family was miserable because of the arranged marriage of her parents. Why would her mother want the same thing for her children?

Tweet had understood at an early age that there was something wrong with her family. She began watching her friends' families not long after that, trying to understand what was different. For instance, most families did not live on opposite sides of their houses and only speak to each other to throw insults.

Chisha was determined to mold Tweet into her image and Tweet didn't want to be her. Once again, she thanked the Gods for her second mother, Larasin. Larasin had given her a chance to escape the stifling company of her mother. Tweet quietly resisted her mother's efforts. She made her own decisions and refused to allow herself to become hateful.

Her brothers were the foundation she'd used to build herself. They had all been very close growing up and it had been horrible after Daeshen had left to start his own life. She had still had Tre'nan, her other brother, to support her and keep her spirits high, but he too had left home for college this year. Sometimes she thought she would go mad without her older brothers to buffer her from her mother's cutting tongue.

She became aware of Thea and Sya'tia watching her curiously and realized she had been sitting there for several minutes without answering them. "Oh, um, I like writing and painting. I haven't decided what I want to study in college. Mother wants me to take government administration courses. I like math and might choose something along those lines."

"Hmmm…" Thea murmured, setting another stitch.

Tweet watched. She didn't recognize the flower Thea was working on. It had multiple petals and was a deep red color. "What is that?" she asked, curiously, not really wanting to talk about herself.

"A rose." Thea looked up and smiled at her. "Embroidery is very relaxing. Would you like to try?"

She nodded eagerly, following Thea with her eyes when the other woman stood and started digging objects out of a bag. A soft hissing sound brought her attention to Sya'tia. She had taken a knife from somewhere and was sharpening the blade with a small stone.

"Your brother is very good at math as well," Sya'tia said softly, not looking up. She tested the edge with her thumb and hummed softly with satisfaction. The blade disappeared and another appeared as if by magic. She set to work on the edge while Tweet watched curiously.

It was a little disconcerting how easily Sya'tia handled the blades. Thea was acting as if there was nothing unusual about someone honing knives in her bedroom. She reached for the same nonchalance. She had never spent time with any of the Chosen and now she had two of them in her family. It was going to take a bit of getting used to.

Thea bustled back over and sat closer to Tweet. She quickly set a scrap of cloth over a hoop and secured it with another hoop. "Have you embroidered before, hon?" she asked, fixing the cloth so it lay just so.

"No," Tweet replied, watching Thea's nimble fingers fly. The cloth had a faint outline of a different kind of flower on it.

Thea set several twisted strands of thread on the table next to them. "This is an iris. I thought you might like it." She picked up a needle and threaded it before handing it and the hoop to Tweet. Then, she picked up her own hoop. "Now, you make the stitches like this. We'll start with the basics and work our way up if you like it."

Tweet's forehead wrinkled as she carefully followed Thea's slow motions. The deep vibrant purple of the thread looked wonderful against the rich cream cloth. She did several more stitches before another hissing sound made her look up.

Sya'tia had put away all her knives and was digging a book out of her belongings. When she settled back down to read, Tweet marveled at how peaceful the companionable silence was. She was so used to silence being an icy thing filled with tension that it took her several moments to realize why she was relaxing. She decided to enjoy it and bent back over her embroidery hoop. It was a little surprising when she realized that she wanted these strong, confident women to like her. *It would be nice to have a real family*, she thought with longing.

An hour passed broken only by the soft sounds of Thea's humming and occasional instruction and Sya'tia turning the pages of her book. Tweet looked at the cover. She jerked back in surprise. The thin, floppy book had a huge blood splattered monster on the cover. Its yellowed teeth dripped drool and its fiery eyes glared malevolently.

"What are you reading?" she asked, horror creeping into her voice.

Sya'tia looked up. "Huh? Oh, it's a magazine Thea had. It's about horror movies on Earth. Good stuff. We'll have to watch a couple." She grinned.

"Horror movies?" Tweet asked cautiously.

Sya'tia leaned forward, her face filling with animation. "They are great! Humans can be very creative about their cinema! And they love to be scared!" She turned to Thea. "We should show her that one movie... *Feast*! That one!"

Thea laughed, not looking up. "I don't think that would be the best movie to start her on, Sya. That's pretty gory and has a lot of inside humor. Maybe *Friday the 13th*? That was my first horror movie."

Tweet watched her set another perfect stitch. She wasn't sure she wanted to watch a horror movie. She opened her mouth to decline but was cut off when the door to the bedroom slammed open.

Chisha glared at them before fixing her daughter with a frigid look. "Young lady, get out of the chair and to your room immediately."

Tweet felt the blood leave her face in a cold rush and bowed her head over her embroidery hoop for a moment to hide her humiliation. In that moment she hated her mother. *I didn't do anything wrong!* she thought to herself miserably, knowing that when she got to her room her mother would give her a tongue-lashing in that frigid voice she used when one of her children had disappointed her. Tweet hated that voice. It was one of her earliest memories of her mother and would probably be the last tone in Chisha's voice when her frozen heart finally stopped beating.

Thea set her hoop in her lap and looked at Chisha calmly. "You may leave now, Chisha. Close the door and do not open it again until you are given permission to do so." Next she looked at Tweet. "You are welcome to stay as long as you wish."

Chisha hissed angrily. "How dare you tell me what to do in my own home?" She snapped her fingers. "Fwa'twee, to your room!"

Thea moved the hoop to the table. "You gave us the use of this room while we abide in your home. Therefore, it is our home until we leave. You have just violated our privacy.

You are the rudest woman I have ever had the misfortune to meet. Sadly, I will have to deal with you for the rest of your life. However, that doesn't mean I have to tolerate your lack of respect. How your family allows you to treat them when I am not around is their business, but how you treat them when I am around is something totally different. Now, as I said before; you may leave." Thea ignored the stunned look on Tweet's face and Sya'tia's stifled giggles.

Chisha's mouth opened and closed like a stranded fish. She turned and walked out of the room. The door shut quietly behind her.

Thea returned to her embroidery and calmly began working on it again while she gave Tweet time to absorb the exchange that had just taken place. Several minutes later she was still staring at Thea in disbelief.

Thea looked at the younger woman and arched an eyebrow. "No one stands up to your mother, do they?" she asked quietly.

Tweet shook her head mutely.

"Hmmm." Thea tilted her head to the side. "They should. If you ignore it, she'll just keep doing it."

Tweet made a noncommittal noise, still staring at Thea. She set aside her embroidery. "I should go." She stood and hurried to the door but paused before opening it. "May I come back?" she asked hesitantly.

Thea and Sya'tia both assured her they would love to spend time with her. Tweet looked quietly pleased as she left.

Sya'tia tossed the magazine aside.

Thea looked at her enquiringly. Her fiancée rubbed her temples.

"Thea, I want to go home. I can't stand her any longer," Sya'tia said quietly. "I don't want to leave you, but I don't think I'll be able to take much more."

Thea sighed softly. Most people didn't realize how sensitive Sya'tia was about her looks. Chisha seemed to home in on a person's weaknesses and threw as much abuse at them as she could. "Then go home, love. I can take her; you shouldn't have to. We can come out after the trial. It's supposed to start in a few days anyway and Kyrin doesn't think it will last more than a few days."

Sya'tia looked distraught. Thea got up and curled herself at Sya'tia's feet. "It's okay, really." She set her chin on the taller woman's knee. "We'll go home soon and everything will be okay. Back to normal, or at least as normal as we get."

"I feel like I'm deserting you," Sya'tia said softly.

"You're not, the guys are still here. Besides, I don't think you're going to be allowed into the courtroom and I don't really want you have to hang out with Chisha." Thea rose up onto her knees and kissed her fiancée lightly. "You might snap and kill her without my calming presence." She winked when Sya'tia laughed softly. "You get packed. We'll tell the guys when they get back from whatever it is they are doing."

Sya'tia nodded. "If you're sure."

"I'm sure," Thea replied with a confidence she didn't feel.

Chapter Twelve

Thea rolled over and looked at Daeshen. He was sound asleep. Everyone else seemed to be able to adjust to the time differences from the ship, but not her. She still woke up at her usual time even though they had been planet-side for over a month.

The bed seemed horribly empty. She felt cranky and hadn't slept well the last couple of nights. Sya'tia had left three days ago and Kyrin had been called back to the ship the next day. The maintenance crews were ready to revolt and Kyrin's bosses wanted to know what was going on.

It was strange how she had become used to them sleeping beside her. Without them, she and Daeshen had clung together in the huge bed.

She pulled out of his arms and stumbled across the room to find the magic jar she had brought from the ship with her. The brown crystals had a faint sheen to them as she stared blearily at them. Coffee. Instant, but it was still coffee.

She quickly threw on some clothes and stumbled from the room and trudged to the kitchen to heat some water.

Several minutes later she was slumped at the kitchen table inhaling the steam from a freshly brewed cup. She took a cautious sip and sighed softly with pleasure. As long as she could have her morning cup in silence she could handle anything. The guys had quickly learned it was best to not speak to her until she poured the second cup. Even Sya'tia gave her a wide berth before that second cup.

Sound seemed to grate on her nerves first thing in the morning. She could wake up in a perfectly good mood and then wham! Insta-bitch! All it took was someone talking to her.

She took another swallow and savored the hot slide of the liquid going down her throat. Faint footsteps sounded in the hall. She glowered into her mug. The morning staff didn't usually come in this early.

Thea didn't look up when someone came into the kitchen. She took another drink.

A thick pile of papers slammed down in front of her. Thea jumped, almost spilling her cup.

"What did you do to make him do it, you little piece of trash?" Chisha screeched shrilly.

Thea flinched as Chisha's harsh voice scraped her ultrasensitive nerves. "I see my moment of solitude will be coming to an end," she said in a sleep-roughened voice. She took another gulp, hoping the caffeine would hit soon because she really didn't want to deal with Daeshen's mother without it. "What seems to be your latest problem, Chisha?"

She and Daeshen had gotten into a huge argument last night because of his mother. He didn't think Thea was putting any effort into getting along. Thea was of the mind that you couldn't talk to someone like that and Chisha could try making an effort too. She'd also said a few things she regretted and planned on apologizing as soon as he woke up. He had fallen asleep with silent tears leaking into her hair.

"This!" Chisha yelled, stabbing a finger at the papers.

Thea pulled them around to see what had her so riled up. She read the first page with dawning horror.

It was the medical and security reports of her attack.

Her body went cold, then hot.

"Where did you get this?" she asked in a hoarse voice.

"That's none of your business," Chisha stated arrogantly.

Thea looked up from the papers slowly; her temples throbbed angrily. "I think it is my business. I want to know how you got copies of these documents."

The older woman smirked triumphantly. "I'm not going to tell you."

Thea set her hands carefully on the table and pushed herself up. "Very well, I'll take it up with the chief of security." She turned to leave the room.

Chisha grabbed her arm and spun her around. "What did you do to make him attack you? It must have been *your* fault. He's a wellborn man. Unlike you, he was raised properly." Her face was filled with haughty disdain.

Thea stilled. Her vision grayed and Chisha's face went out of focus. "My fault..." she said softly. "You think it's my fault." She struggled to bring the older woman back into focus. "That man raped four women. He admitted to it in front of witnesses."

Chisha blew a raspberry at Thea and waved her hand airily. "Human women. Obviously they were doing something to taunt him."

"You must be joking," Thea said slowly.

"Of course I'm not joking." Chisha rolled her eyes.

Thea took a deep breath, and then she pointed to her face. "Do you see these marks?" She traced the scars that outlined her God-marks.

"Yes, what the Gods were thinking I have no idea."

Thea unbuttoned her shirt and spread it open to bare the top of her chest. "Do you see these blackened spots?"

Chisha's mouth tightened. "Yes, and I would appreciate it if you covered yourself. That's disgraceful! We are in the kitchen!"

Thea gritted her teeth for a moment. "That is where Barik tried to skin me alive. The asana don't know if the marks will ever fade. After he finished that he was going to cut out my eyes." She buttoned the shirt again. "He killed my baby. Your first grandchild."

Chisha's face paled but she waved her hand dismissively again. "I'm sure it was Kyrin's child. Or, maybe it was Barik's and that's why he was angry."

Thea's mouth dropped open. After a speechless moment she shut it with a snap. She shook her head slowly. "You have all the compassion of a serial killer," she said in a horrified voice.

"I would have to agree," said a new voice. They both jumped and turned toward it.

Daeshen stood in the doorway staring at his mother like he had never seen her before. A taller man stood behind him. His hair was very similar to Daeshen's but much shorter and had more green in the blue. His face was a mask of horror.

Daeshen took an uncertain step toward his mother. "Who are you? To think I yelled at Thea last night because she wasn't trying to get along with you." He turned to look at his wife. "Has she been like this the whole time?"

Chisha had been careful to save her most cutting remarks for when Daeshen and Kyrin weren't present. Not that she had been pleasant when they were around. But she had never said enough to make the men feel they had to intervene.

Thea nodded. "I'm not staying here any longer, Daeshen. I don't care what rules of etiquette I'm breaking. I can't do this anymore. If I have to look at her over another dinner table I'm going to stab her with my fork."

"Go pack, love. We're leaving." Daeshen met his mother's eyes squarely. "And we are not coming back. My children will not be subjected to this. It's obvious how you will treat our 'half-breed mongrels,'" he said quietly.

Chisha paled. "Daeshen..."

He turned around and left without another word. Thea followed him.

Chapter Thirteen

The man with Daeshen cleared his throat as he followed them up the stairs to their room. Thea glanced at him sideways, wondering who he was and a little embarrassed he had witnessed the argument in the kitchen.

She tried to send a small push of curiosity to Daeshen, hoping he would remember to introduce her. He looked at her for a moment, his brow creasing faintly.

She nudged him gently and slid a sideways look at the stranger.

Daeshen blushed. "I'm sorry, love." He paused. "Thea, this is my brother, Tre'nan."

Tre'nan nodded and smiled briefly.

Thea murmured a greeting. She was really showing off her best side to Daeshen's family. So far they had all seen her get in a snarkfest with Chisha at one time or another. Classy.

They reached the bedroom and Daeshen immediately began throwing his clothing into bags. His jerky movements were filled with suppressed anger.

Thea turned to Tre'nan. "I'm sorry you had to witness that," she said softly. "It has been a trying week. It's a pleasure to meet you." She held her hands out to him.

He smiled and took them, leaning forward to press a kiss to her cheek. "Don't worry; I am well aware of my esteemed first mother's faults."

Thea touched his hair gently. "Your hair is so short." She smiled when several tendrils curled around her fingers and tightened gently.

He laughed. "That's because I just turned nineteen." He turned to Daeshen. "Haven't you told her anything about us?" His hair released her fingers as he turned back to her. "Our hair grows long about a year after we reach sexual maturity." He leered playfully. "Must be all those hormones needing somewhere to go. Mine should start growing soon," he said with a grin. "I'm an early bloomer."

Thea blushed, embarrassed by her ignorance. She had been curious but hadn't mentioned it before. Now that she thought about it, all the children she had seen had shoulder-length hair. "Oh," she murmured.

He turned and started pulling the clothing back out of the bags and began folding it neatly. "Calm down, Dae. Do it properly. Better yet, why don't you call a hotel and make a reservation while Thea and I pack and get to know each other?"

Daeshen stared down at the shirt he had crumpled in his hands. He let it fall onto the bed with a sigh. "I never thought she would be like this, Tre. I knew she was sniping at Thea and Sya'tia. She never said much to Kyrin because he was a male and not that important to her." He turned to Thea, tears swimming in his eyes. "Can you forgive me, darling?"

Thea went to him and hugged him tight. His arms wrapped around her convulsively. "Always, love. Besides, some of it is my fault. You were right last night; I could have made more of an effort. I'm sorry for the things I said to you."

He looked deeply into her eyes. "Who would have thought you would be so strong? You are so delicate. We chose well." He pressed a kiss to her lips. "You are like a meecha protecting us."

Thea pulled back so she could see his face. "What the hell is a meecha? Sya'tia kept saying Chisha had a mouth like one."

Tre'nan barked out a laugh. He busied himself with the clothes when Thea glanced at him.

Daeshen laughed softly. "She does have a mouth like a meecha. They are a predator more deadly than your great white sharks. They have teeth shaped like, uh..." He seemed to grope for the right words. "Round saw blades. They spin" -- he twirled his finger -- "and there are three sets. When they eat something it just disappears. Bones, hair, scales, everything. It's just gone."

Thea blanched as he demonstrated with his hands. These creatures had grinders for mouths. "Holy crap. Are they mean?"

Tre'nan spoke up, "Not really. They are very gentle, but territorial. We try to avoid them because they have never been very receptive to us. It is said that they lived here before the Ta'e'sha." He turned to face Thea, his face full of animation. "I'm going to study them when I finish college! There's so much we don't know about them. They have a rudimentary type of psychic ability we don't understand. They use it in conjunction with body language, I think. My professor is very interested in my theories; she says I have fresh ideas." He beamed.

"That's great! What do they look like?" She rubbed slow circles on Daeshen's back, silently urging him to relax. She cuddled closer, letting him take comfort in her touch.

Tre'nan fairly bounced with enthusiasm. "They have small hollow bones like a bird, but each bone is tiny, no bigger than the tip of your finger. This makes them light and streamlined in the water, but they can also fly short distances in the air. The way their bones fit together gives them a range of motion completely different from ours. Every bone is jointed so they can move in ripples. They have short brown fur that is lighter and darker in unique patterns. I have pictures in my room I can show you. They are beautiful! And so fluid in the water that you would weep to watch them. They live in small colonies and seem to farm several types of fish."

"They farm? Really?" Thea couldn't think of any animals that farmed. She vaguely remembered some speculation that certain types of dinosaurs had a rudimentary form of farming, but their colleagues had laughed the scientists who had thought up the theory out of the field. She felt Daeshen bury his face in her neck and smile against her skin. He was relaxing as he listened to her talk with his brother.

"I think so," Tre'nan looked uncertain. "My professor says that it is a wild idea and to keep my mind open when I begin studying them because I might get so caught up in the idea that I won't see anything else."

"That's good advice. It's easy to see what you want to be there instead of what is actually there," she replied. "Just look at them like you have never seen them before and you might learn more than you could imagine."

A knock on the doorjamb made them all look. Tweet stood in the threshold, her eyes fixed hungrily on Tre'nan. "Can I come in?" she asked softly.

"Of course," Daeshen replied.

Tweet gave them a blinding smile before launching herself at Tre'nan, who quickly caught her up in a bear hug.

"I've missed you!" she sang, kissing her brother's cheeks. "When did you arrive? How is school? Are you dating anyone? What classes are you taking? Did you bring me a present?" The words burst from her. She kept hugging and kissing her brother.

Tre'nan laughed and twirled her around the room. "Just now, it's good, no, biology and yes."

Thea had no idea how he remembered all that. She glanced up at her husband who was beaming at his younger siblings. In that moment Thea didn't care about Chisha; she was just glad she had met her husband's brother and sister. She still hadn't met his father or second mother, but, she thought, he must be quite a man to raise such wonderful children in spite of his evil-tongued wife.

Tweet was giggling when Tre'nan set her down. He pulled a small package out of his back pocket and presented it to her with a flourish. She beamed and ripped the paper off it. It fell to the ground like snowflakes as she opened the box inside.

She gasped with pleasure as she pulled free a small pendant on a braided cord. "It's so pretty! Thank you, Tre!" She quickly put it on. "Look, Thea, it's a chrystarea!"

Thea took a closer look. The pendant was made of glass and contained swirls of colored glass. It was a small flower. The center was a deep purple. Five petals flowed out from it; wide and curving, they began as a pale peach and deepened to pink and then narrowing into spiraling tips of blood red.

"It's beautiful," she murmured.

"They only bloom once every seven years," Tweet informed her, still admiring it. After several moments she looked up and finally noticed the bags. "Where are you going?"

Daeshen cleared his throat. "We are going to stay at a hotel until the trial is completed."

Tweet went very still. She carefully examined Thea and then Daeshen. "What happened?" she asked quietly.

"Better you don't know, hon," Thea broke in before Daeshen could say anything. "Some things are best left alone, okay?"

Tweet nodded slowly, her face still full of questions. "May I visit you again? I would like to learn more embroidery."

"Of course," Thea said, hugging the girl. "I would be delighted. As soon as I know where we are going I'll have Daeshen let you know, all right?"

The girl nodded and smiled shakily before turning to trail out of the room. She stopped at the door and turned back to Thea. "I would like to learn weaving, sister. Will you teach me?"

Thea nodded gravely. "I'll get what you will need tomorrow, love."

"Thank you." Tweet smiled again, with more confidence, before leaving them.

Tre'nan was watching her curiously when she turned to help him fold clothes. "What?" she asked self-consciously.

But all he said was, "My sister likes you."

"I like her too," she replied and changed the subject back to meechas.

Chapter Fourteen

Thea nervously brushed an imaginary speck off the severe black suit she was wearing. Her fingers trembled slightly and she quickly clasped them together. She and her husbands were waiting to be called into the courtroom, as were the other women who had been attacked by Barik.

The women all had a faintly sick cast to their features and their husbands seemed torn between anger, sadness, and fear. The ramifications of today's trial would echo through the Ta'e'shian culture for a long time.

They all jumped when the door swung open. A guard stepped out and announced they were to come in and take their seats. The men guided their wives into a huge room barren of softening décor. The seats were heavy wooden benches with very little carving to soften their imposing build. The walls were painted a soft gray with lighter gray marbling.

Life-size statues of the God and Goddess of Balance stood with regal dignity in each corner of the room. Their blank eyes seemed to watch the room soberly.

At the front of the room eleven people sat behind a long curved table. A high asana of each sex represented each of the temples. A still, imposing woman sat in the center. The sight of her made all the Ta'e'shian men draw in a startled breath and quickly bow toward her respectfully. She nodded regally in return.

She had her hair twisted into an ornate set of twining braids. Her skin and hair were a light golden yellow with a faint sheen. Her eyes glistened like newly minted gold coins as she watched the room without expression. She wore a dark gold robe embroidered heavily with the symbols of the Lithen, Gods and Goddesses of their race.

Daeshen had told Thea that because of Barik's place in the royal families, a member of the Royal Council would probably be present for the hearing and trial. As she watched, a younger version of the woman slipped quietly out of a side room and silently took a place behind and to the left of the woman. The newcomer did not have the same expressionless visage, but she tried. She was dressed in a less ornate set of robes with the same set of symbols. Her coloring was the exact shades of the woman seated at the center of the table.

Thea looked at the other people in the room. All of the guards were Warrior Chosen. They were dressed in black livery with dark gold trim and a gold wave crest over the left breast. Two guards stood at each door and four guards stood at attention behind the Council. Several people were seated along other benches, there to witness the hearing and trial.

An older woman with the same features and coloring as Barik sat like carved marble. Her mouth was compressed into a tight line. Her eyes were glassy with emotion. Far in the back of the room Daeshen's mother sat. Her gaze was cold as it collided with Thea's. She sighed to herself in resignation. There didn't seem to be any hope that Chisha could ever accept Thea's place in Daeshen's life, let alone like her. Her own actions had probably made the situation worse, but Thea couldn't live her life trying to make everyone else happy. Besides, if she gave an inch, Chisha would take a mile and still bitch about it.

Two guards escorted Barik into the chamber and sat him at a table along the wall opposite Thea and the other women. He glared at them with baleful hatred.

A choked sob sounded behind her. She did not turn to see who it was. It was all she could do to keep from crying herself. The blood drained from her face in a cold rush, leaving her pale and trembling.

An assistant of the courts stood and called the hearing to order. "Please stand while the Council is announced and the charges are read." The occupants of the room stood. The assistant named the members of the asana. "Judgment shall be passed at the end of this trial by Shayateen, High Queen of Ta'e."

Thea's head reeled. The High Queen would be passing judgment? What would that mean? Why was she showing an interest? She pulled her attention back to the charges the assistant was listing. Her husbands trembled as the list ended with the death of their child, miscarried due to the beating Thea had received.

Other than a tightening of her lips, the High Queen remained expressionless through the recital of charges. The older woman in the audience, identified as Barik's mother, sobbed softly and covered her eyes with one hand. She turned blindly to the man beside her. He put his arm around her shoulders, his features tight and gray with grief.

The hours passed slowly as each woman was called forward and questioned by the asana. The impact of their shuddering, terrified answers was seen on the faces of the asana asking the questions and the people watching the proceedings. After each woman was questioned, evidence was presented to the Council.

Unlike human courts, they would not be dismissed until all the victims were heard from; then, depending on the time, Barik would be questioned and the verdict would be given the next day. Much of the legal wrangling so common in Earth courts was missing and as a result the hearing passed much faster.

Finally, late in the afternoon, Thea was called before the Council. As she stood and walked toward the table where she would sit, two points of light appeared before the table and slowly coalesced into two human forms.

Their eyes were black as night and their hair faded from pale blond to the rich brown of newly turned earth and finally to silvery white before beginning the cycle again.

The Council gasped.

Skye and Gaia turned and smiled gently at Thea who quickly knelt before them.

"Rise, daughter."

She straightened and stood, her gaze downcast respectfully.

They turned back to the Council. Gaia spoke. "Forgive Our intrusion. We come on behalf of Our daughter, Theadora."

The High Queen swallowed visibly before speaking. "What would you have of us, *Lith* of Theadora Auralel?" It was the first time she had spoken through the entire proceeding. Her voice was low and heavy with the vibrations common to her race. It was the quality that gave them the ability to ensnare the human mind. Kyrin had told her that the High Queen had the ability to halt a mob if she chose to exert her full vocal range. It was a trait that always appeared in one of the Queen's daughters each generation and denoted who would be heir to the throne.

"We have come to give Our testimony as witness of the attack on Our daughter, as she requested during the attack," Skye replied gravely.

The High Queen nodded slowly in response. "Please proceed."

Gaia turned and faced Skye. "We would show you. A picture is worth one thousand words, as Our daughter would say." She raised her hands, palms out to Skye, who copied the motion. The room was silent other than the fast breathing of the shocked audience.

The air shimmered gently between their hands, and after a moment, an image of Thea walking in a hallway appeared, her hand cradled her stomach and a small smile graced her lips.

Barik's mother cried out as the God and Goddess showed Barik slip up silently behind Thea and inject her with paralytic venom. Every moment of the attack was shown to the Council and every other person in the room in clear, brutal, detail. Every word that spewed from his lips made the men and women listening flinch. Several women sobbed as they watched the beating, Thea's rescue, and entrance to the medical center. Thea moaned as she watched her child emerge into the world, already dead, not even identifiable as a child. The scenes ended with Kyrin and Daeshen huddled around Thea's still form. Her eyes stared blankly as tears leaked from the corners in silvery trails.

Tears streamed down Thea's cheeks and she struggled to breathe with lungs that felt too small. She had felt every moment and relived the trauma again. She was embarrassed so many people had witnessed her humiliation and pain.

A member of the asana cleared his throat. "You may return to your seat, Theadora Auralel, I do not think we will need to ask you any questions." He swallowed convulsively.

She nodded gratefully and returned to her husbands, who immediately cuddled her between them. One of the other victims touched her shoulder. Thea met her tear-filled gaze and shuddered at the compassion and understanding she found there.

Skye and Gaia nodded to the queen and Council before taking seats near Thea. Their eyes slowly faded from black to gray.

The other women edged back a bit, eyeing the God and Goddess warily. Their husbands nodded respectfully, but without fear.

As the assistant began to call for Barik to give his testimony and defense, two more lights appeared before the Council. They formed into the God and Goddess of Warriors. The Ta'e'sha quickly stood and knelt in Their presence.

Except Barik. He lounged back in his seat and glared at them insolently.

Kashka looked at the Council for a moment. "We would not interfere were We not also attacked by this man. We would draw it to the attention of the Council that Theadora would not have been attacked had she not been marked by

Us. His actions insulted Us and shamed him. He harmed these women, Our nieces, for things they could have no control over and were not to blame for. We will make reparation to these women. We wish Our children to make reparation to them as well."

Vosh nodded. He looked directly at the High Queen and spoke. "Do not return to Earth for more women. We accept the ladies Our sons have taken into their hearts, but you will not tear more women away from all they know. Barik has taken the extreme attitude of what already floats through the minds of others. Do what must be done, daughter; only you have the power and influence to do so."

They both faded away silently.

Shayateen shivered then composed her face back into a blank mask. She motioned for the assistant to approach her and whispered in his ear for a moment.

He nodded and turned to face the room. "We will be adjourning early this evening and will continue tomorrow morning at the same time. At which time the defendant will be heard from. Thank you for your time, ladies and gentlemen."

People began gathering their belongings and slowly filing out. As instructed beforehand, Thea and the other women waited until the room was empty before leaving.

Skye and Gaia stood and faded quietly away.

* * *

Thea ran for the bathroom again. She made it just in time and vomited convulsively. Her empty stomach continued to vainly expel the taint Thea felt from having to watch the attack. They had returned directly to their hotel room after the hearing. Watching Daeshen quietly weep while Kyrin paced the generous confines of the room like a caged tiger had not helped the nausea. It helped even less that their child's casket had been very carefully placed in the evidence. All during the hearing Thea had been aware of its presence. The Council had informed Kyrin that they wanted it displayed to impress upon those watching of the gravity of the charges being brought against Barik. Thea was sickened and horrified that her baby was an object, a tool, to them. She wanted, *needed*, her child to be laid to rest. She had wondered bitterly if they would have halted the rites of a fully Ta'e'shian child.

The heaves slowed and then finally stopped, and Thea leaned weakly against the toilet. She finally flushed the contents and dragged herself upright to rinse her mouth. After staring at her haggard face in the mirror for a few minutes, she dug a small bottle out of her toiletry bag. She quickly swallowed one of the small purple tablets it held and then shook out two more.

Walking back into the bedroom she offered them to her husbands. "Hey, Corvin gave me these before we left the ship. He said it's a mild sedative. We need to eat dinner then go to bed." She wiped the tears from Daeshen's cheeks. "The hearing will start early tomorrow."

Kyrin refused with an angry shake of his head. "I don't want to relax. I want to feel his blood sliding over my hands like a river."

Thea went to him and curled her arms around his waist, resting her head on his chest. "Stop," she whispered softly. "It will be over soon and then we can move on." She didn't know how long it would take, but she would get beyond what had happened to her. His arms slid around her, his muscles trembling with tension. "I know it hurts, Kyrin, but you have to let it go."

He buried his face in her hair, his breath warm against her scalp. "How can I let it go, Thea?" he whispered raggedly. "I saw it all; those images will never leave me. I know how much it hurt you; still hurts you."

Thea rubbed his back soothingly while her own stomach roiled. "Time is the great healer, my husband. Let it do its work. If you don't, it will fester and rip us apart." She felt Daeshen join them, his arms sliding around them both.

After several minutes, Kyrin relaxed and let them comfort him. "As soon as this is done we're going to Sya's home, right?" she asked eventually. Since Sya'tia wasn't yet married to them she had been excluded from the people allowed into the hearing. She would really like to know how Chisha had managed to get in. And she intended to find out as soon as she had time.

Daeshen nodded against her neck, where his face was buried.

"Good. You two can swim and help her family with the farm; the water will help center you." They had another two months before they left again. Kyrin had just informed them they would be returning to Earth to gather more samples while other ships were sent to begin the terraforming of the planets chosen by the Gods. There were enough basic samples for them to begin building a breathable atmosphere, which was the first, and longest, step in building a habitable world.

She kissed Kyrin's jaw gently. The sedative was doing its work and her stomach was calming quickly. Her husbands caressed her gently, their hands roaming over her small frame. Their touches weren't sexual; it was more that they were trying to reassure themselves she was whole and alive. They had always been free with affection, but since the attack there was a searching quality to it. It was one of the many small changes that had taken place.

There was a quiet knock at the door.

Kyrin untangled himself from the arms of his mates and went to answer.

The opening door revealed Chisha standing uncomfortably in the hall. Thea watched her narrowly as Kyrin bade her to enter. Her hair, so like her son's, was clenched in an uncomfortable-looking knot at the back of her neck. She met Thea's gaze for a moment before skittering to a chair and sitting down.

Daeshen's arms tightened around her. She knew he wasn't looking forward to another round of arguing between his wife and his mother. Childish though it was, Thea consoled herself with thinking, *She started it.*

Chisha drew herself up in the chair and addressed Thea with rigid formality. "I came to apologize for my behavior regarding the attack made upon your person by Barik. I have realized you did not do anything to warrant such actions." She stood and carefully smoothed her clothing. "I realize I have overstepped myself and hope that you can forgive me and we can learn to be friends." She had the look of a woman who expected her words to be thrown back in her face. She reminded Thea of Ruri in that moment. *This is what Ruri could become. Maybe I should drag her down here to spend*

*a week or two with Chisha. It might straighten both of them
out a bit. Or kill them.*

Thea eyed her warily. She ignored the hopeful tension in
Daeshen's body as she studied his mother. "And Sya'tia?" she
asked finally. She wasn't willing to let Chisha start treating
her better if she was going to continue being a bitch to
Sya'tia.

Chisha's eyes flinched slightly. "I will accept her into my
family."

It was not the warmest declaration Thea had ever heard,
but she'd take what she could get. "Would you care to join us
for dinner?" she finally asked. Chisha looked surprised by the
offer. Thea suspected the older woman expected to be kicked
out.

Chisha nodded her acceptance. "I would like that, thank
you."

* * *

The next morning Thea dressed carefully in black slacks
and a dark gray silk blouse. Her silver pentagram rested
against her skin, just below her collarbones, shining gently in
the light. She pulled her hair back into a neat French braid
and took a deep breath. She turned to face the guys. Daeshen
had copied her hairstyle. It was an interesting look; he was
almost too pretty for words. Luckily, she had managed to talk
him out of the bow. She made a mental note to cut his anime
watching. It was starting to affect his appearance.

Kyrin was sitting in a chair with a look on his face that
said he was festering with hate. Daeshen looked sad, but
resigned.

"Kyrin, quit killing Barik in your head. Daeshen, straighten the front of your shirt. It's buttoned wrong. Let's go, guys," Thea said briskly, picking up her purse.

Kyrin looked up. His wife look cool and composed, but he knew it was a lie. He could feel her emotions twisting around her. She still hadn't managed to completely shield Daeshen and him from them. It was disconcerting sometimes, but wonderful at other times. He knew how hard it had been for her to view her attack yesterday and was worried his and Daeshen's reaction had been part of the reason she had vomited so many times. He hated to think they were adding to what was already a very difficult situation for her.

The images that had been in his head about how the attack took place had been bad enough. Seeing it was much worse. He was tearing himself apart with guilt that he hadn't been any help. That someone else had saved her. He hadn't even known something was wrong. Logically, he knew there was little way he could have connected his illness during the attack to Thea being hurt, but his heart wasn't logical.

His heart told him he hadn't protected his family. It told him his child had died because he had failed. His heart didn't care that his wife and husband didn't blame him. His heart told him *he* should have saved his wife. Not some security officers who barely knew her name.

He stood and followed them out of the room, trying to leash his emotions. His wife had more than enough to deal with.

Several minutes later they arrived at the Courthouse and he paid the driver. He curled his arm protectively around his wife's waist and ignored the polite questions being asked by reporters waiting outside the building. While there wasn't the media frenzy he had seen in some Earth movies, there was some coverage about the attacks. Very little information had been leaked to the media, only that a member of a royal clan was on trial and that several human women were seen coming and going from the building.

The court was trying to keep the trial as quiet as possible until it was concluded. Then, a dry factual address would be given.

They arrived outside the room and took seats to wait. Kyrin checked the time and noted they were several minutes early and the first to arrive. The other families began trailing in soon after they sat down.

He was surprised when Corvin came in and sat next to him. "What are you doing here?"

The older man sighed. "I was called last night to verify some of the medical facts and testify that Barik did not have access to them and explain my findings on the changes he made to the cerebcoms. Kyaness will be here too. They want to know why Barik's brain patterns were not caught during the mental imbalance scans. She's a stickler; her temple was performing the scans twice a day at random times and they never caught anything off from him."

Kyrin grunted thoughtfully. That was very odd. He hoped Kyaness had answers.

As he continued to talk to Corvin, whom he hadn't seen in a few weeks, he was aware of one of the other women approaching Thea hesitantly. He looked over as she bent down to whisper something in Thea's ear. His wife jerked as if she had been stung and looked up at the woman in surprise. He started to stand and was surprised when a hand clamped down on his wrist. He looked down at it then up at Corvin.

"You're doing it again."

"Doing what?" he grumbled, knowing very well what his friend was talking about.

"Trying to keep the world away from Thea. You have to stop doing that. If you don't, she's going to beat on your thick skull with one of her books. A big one," Corvin replied easily, letting go of Kyrin's wrist. "And then I'll have to patch you up and you'll get pissed, because I'm going to laugh my ass off the whole time I'm doing it." He leaned back and rested his head against the wall. "Besides, that's Giana. She was the last one Barik attacked before Thea. By that point he had...refined...his technique. "

Kyrin blanched. He looked more closely at the woman. She was tall and had dark hair with lighter streaks framing her face. Her skin was also dark with what would normally be a smooth olive complexion. Today it was more of a waxy sallow shade. Her features were pinched and she looked ready to shatter. She was a pretty woman, an exotic beauty by Ta'e'shian standards, but the strain of what had happened to her was slowly leaching the life and beauty from her face.

Thea stared at Giana steadily. "You would be doing it for the wrong reasons."

"That's really not your decision to make, is it?" the other woman replied.

"Not really, but I still think you need to think about it a lot harder before you decide." Thea took the other woman's arm and drew her away from the other people in the room. "Look, Giana, you've been through a huge trauma, but changing your religion isn't going to make it better," she said softly.

"Thea, I've always been Catholic and not once have I had the feeling anyone was listening to me. I've prayed all my life, and nothing… Do you really think a loving God would let this happen?" Giana asked faintly, her eyes were slightly glazed. "But I live my life by His word and I'm kidnapped, married to a complete stranger, and then raped by a sick bastard who thinks his problems are my fault! Sure, you were kidnapped, but your God and Goddess helped you! They intervened! *They care what happens to you!* They even show up at the freaking trial!" She panted slightly, her hands tightened into fists. "I want that. I *need* that!"

Thea took Giana's hand and looked her straight in the eye. "They would not have stopped Barik from raping me. They didn't send the security team that caught him. It was pure chance I was found, Giana. But that is beside the point. There's a reason it's called faith. Just because He doesn't talk to you doesn't mean He's not real! It's not faith if you only do it when it's easy! You need Him now more than ever." She stroked the woman's cheek. "You should look at this as proof that your faith isn't false. If the Lord and Lady are real then there is no reason your God isn't too! Don't give up now, babe, because I'm sure He's been with you every step of the way!"

Giana's lip trembled and tears filled her eyes. Thea pulled her into a tight hug and the taller woman's arms closed convulsively around her. She sobbed softly against Thea's shoulder. "I just want something solid to believe in. I feel so isolated! I can't do this! I want to go home!" she whispered in a watery voice.

Thea rocked her gently. "You're not alone, Giana. You can come see me anytime, and that tall drink of water with purple hair you're married to looks like he'd chew through concrete to get close to you again." She eyed Giana's husband who was glaring daggers at her right now. She motioned him over with a crooked finger, not letting go of Giana. "Just talk to God, pour it all out and give it up to Him. Sometimes when my Gods talk to me, it's nothing more than feeling a little warmer than I did before. They can be subtle; you have to look for the answers."

Giana nodded against her shoulder. Her husband reached them in a few long strides; he started to touch Giana's shoulder but stopped and looked at Thea helplessly. It was obvious that he was wavering between being angry with her for making his wife cry and not knowing if Giana would accept his offer of comfort.

Thea's empathic abilities flared to life and she felt Giana's pain as if it were her own. She felt the blood drain from her face, but tried to draw some of it away from the other woman the way Kyaness had been teaching her. It was like cutting into her own body. The pain was singular.

She gently turned Giana toward her husband, whose name she didn't know. "I think this guy could use a hug, babe."

Giana looked up and smiled wanly at her husband. Her face was streaked with tears, but she bravely held up her arms for a hug.

He was quick to take advantage of it and sent Thea a grateful look before burying his face in his wife's hair.

She quietly slipped back to her husbands and sat beside them. Daeshen put an arm around her shoulders and she leaned tiredly against him. The day hadn't even begun and she was already exhausted.

"What was that all about?" he asked quietly.

"Crisis of faith," she replied just as softly. "Giana wants answers and she's willing to turn to anything she thinks will give them to her."

Daeshen sighed softly and pressed a kiss against her temple.

The doors to the courtroom opened and a guard motioned for them to come in. There was some shuffling as everyone entered and took seats. After everyone was settled, the doors opened to admit the people who would sit in the gallery to watch the proceedings.

Next, Barik was ushered to his place and two guards took positions behind him. That was new. Yesterday they hadn't been there. Thea wondered what had changed. She turned to look at Giana, who sent her a wobbly smile and clutched her husband's hand tightly.

They all stood as the court assistant announced the asana and High Queen again. For some reason it wasn't as hard to look at him today as it was yesterday. Maybe she was going numb. Or maybe she was finally taking the advice she had been flinging at everyone else. Letting it go.

Corvin was the first to be called before the asana. They asked him several questions about how the cerebcoms had been modified and if there would be any lasting effects. Thea was relieved to hear that there would not be. Corvin had managed to repair the damage caused and reprogram the coms so they could not be tampered with again.

Next, Kyaness was called by the court regarding the scans the asana did to monitor the mental health of the residents of the ship. She produced a holoreader that had records of every scan she had done from the time the *Dark Queen* left dock to their return to Ta'e. She was not sure how Barik managed to evade the scanning. It should have pinpointed him the moment his rage grew to the point that he was even thinking about attacking someone. Several of the court asana talked amongst themselves for several minutes before they dismissed Kyaness.

Finally, they called Barik up to give his account of his actions.

Thea braced herself. He looked unkempt, his clothing wrinkled and stained. She wondered if he was refusing to bathe in protest. She knew for a fact the prisons on Ta'e were very carefully managed. She had researched it when she'd arrived. It was a spa compared to what people would have lived with on Earth, but then, the Ta'e'sha didn't have the same type of crimes usually seen on Earth. The harshest part of their prisons was that inmates were kept in solitary confinement through most of their sentence. For two hours during the day they were allowed to interact with other inmates and exercise. For another hour they met with an asana to discuss their crime, and the rest of the time they were left to meditate on their actions.

Barik smeared a glare across the women he had victimized before turning to face the court. "I refuse to make excuses for my actions. You brought this about yourselves." He glared at the High Queen with hatred.

She raised an eyebrow, but made no comment.

He continued to rant and rave. Most of it was incoherent. He threw wild accusations at both his own people and the human women with the disregard of a child throwing rocks into a lake. His anger and hatred seemed to stem from people having the gall to be *happy* while his sister lay dead. His world had stopped when she drew her last breath. Why hadn't it stopped for everyone else? Their joy and laughter *mocked his pain!*

When he tried to approach the table the guards quickly restrained him. Barik went insane then, screaming and kicking out at the asana and the High Queen. He spit on the table and bit one of the guards.

The asana look appalled. Even the queen wasn't able to keep her face expressionless in the face of such a display. She looked horrified.

The High Priest of the Temple of Mental Balance cleared his throat after the guards had wrestled Barik back into his chair. "There is no disturbance on the mental plane. It's as if he is calm and thinking about the weather! We shall check into how this is possible, my queen. Perhaps the Gods will be able to tell us more. We shall pray on it."

"They are not my Gods!" Barik screamed, spittle flying from his mouth. "I will never pray to them again! I want no part of Gods who let their children suffer so and claim those filthy whores as their own!"

The High Queen leaned forward and opened her mouth, but quickly shut it again when Gaia and Skye appeared in front of the table.

"Your renouncement has been heard and witnessed," Gaia announced with malevolent glee. "We claim you as restitution for Our daughter's suffering and the life of her child, Robin."

Red balls of light appeared between Gaia, Skye, and Barik. They formed into Kysout and Samonan, God and Goddess of Soul Renewal. Their matched red colors glowed in the light of the room. The Ta'e'sha scrambled out of their chairs and onto their knees.

"You can't claim him! He is still Our child!" Samonan snarled, her hair and fins flaring widely around her.

"He has renounced you, Sister," Skye returned calmly. "Our claim carries the weight of Balance."

Thea's eyes widened as she wondered a bit wildly if she was going to witness a Deity Smackdown Cage Match.

Kysout nodded meditatively. "It does, Brother. However, he still has a choice." He turned to face Barik. "Child, you have a choice before you. Accept Us once again and be at peace in your next cycle. Or remain as you are. We cannot go against the claim made by Gaia and Skye for it was made after you renounced Us, but after your death you will go to them unless you take Us back into your heart."

"I want nothing to do with you. I hate you; the very sight of you sickens me!" Barik growled hoarsely.

Samonan keened softly. Thea's heart jumped painfully in her breast at the sound of the Goddess's sadness.

Kysout nodded sadly. "Your choice has been made, witnessed, and enacted. You are not Our child. We are no longer responsible for your care."

They both faded slowly away, watching Barik with tears trailing down their cheeks.

"We love you, child," Samonan whispered softly as the last traces of red wisped away.

Thea let out the breath she had been holding. She slid a glance at Barik's mother. The poor woman looked shattered. She was swaying in place where she sat in the gallery. Her eyes were blind as she stared at her son as if she had never seen him before. Thea didn't think she wanted to know what she was thinking. She had no idea how she would be able to watch this if it had been her child sitting in that chair.

Gaia turned to Skye and smiled slowly. Then she turned to face the asana and High Queen. "We realize this is highly irregular, but We do not feel your court or society would be able to create a fit punishment for these crimes."

The High Queen studied the deities silently for a moment. "We have witnessed Barik's care pass from our Gods' hands and into Yours, Lord and Lady. Punish him as you see fit," she said quietly, her voice rolling like velvet across the listeners.

Barik's mother let out a choked cry of protest.

Skye nodded gravely. "Thank you. We understand this was not a decision made lightly."

The High Queen nodded slowly in response.

Gaia approached Thea and the other women. "Daughter and nieces, We would like to take some of your pain away first."

Thea stood up and knelt before her Lady. Giana was the second to come forward. She started to kneel as well, but Gaia stopped her with gentle hands on her arms. "You do not have to kneel, darling. You do not worship Us and We would not ask you to compromise your own beliefs."

Giana nodded slowly, looking at the floor. Claudette and Joyce stood next to her. They looked relieved they would not have to kneel. Sarah was the last to join them.

Gaia smiled softly at the nervous women as she helped Thea rise. "Ladies, your faith is never groundless; someone is always listening." Her gaze paused for a moment on Giana's face.

Skye came to stand behind Gaia. He smiled encouragingly at the nervous women.

Thea watched as Gaia moved to stand before Claudette. She touched a single long, graceful finger to Claudette's forehead. Claudette shuddered for a moment and then relaxed. When Gaia removed her finger and moved to Sarah, Claudette swayed tiredly.

The Goddess repeated the action with Joyce and Giana who all had similar responses. They shuddered and turned pale before drooping with exhaustion.

Thea looked up at her Lady without fear. She closed her eyes when that cool fingertip touched her forehead. Suddenly every action Barik had taken, every violation, swirled wildly through her brain. Then it melted away. It was not completely gone, but now it was fuzzy around the edges, as if it had happened years ago and to someone else. She was able to look at the memory without sweat breaking out on her body and feeling cold to the bone.

She sighed softly at the sudden release of tension from her muscles. She hadn't realized how tight she had been holding her body. It was magic. It was wonderful. She smiled gratefully up at her Goddess, who returned the smile tenderly.

As one, the God and Goddess moved to Barik.

Skye looked around the room before focusing his attention on Barik, who finally seemed to realize what he had done. "Barik, brother of Balai, you have been found guilty of the crimes of rape, torture, and murder. Your punishment shall be to live with your actions for the rest of your life."

Barik smirked, obviously not finding that a hardship.

Skye moved behind him and motioned the guards to step away. He grasped Barik's arms and nodded to Gaia.

Barik started to look nervous again and began to struggle when Gaia reached toward him with the same finger that had touched the women.

It did no good; Skye held him easily.

Gaia touched Barik's forehead.

Barik stilled, then began to convulse and howl with agony. It was several minutes before Gaia lifted her fingertip away from him. He screamed and thrashed against the God's hands. Skye released him and Barik slid from the chair and began clawing at his body. His screams of agony turned into terrified shrieks.

Both Gods watched him dispassionately. "Every day you shall relive each attack, each fear, every moment of pain. You will experience their terror and the death of Theadora's child. You will know what it is to live through it as one of your victims." They spoke in unison, their forms beginning to glow with white light. "Every moment will be for you as it was for them. For the rest of your life."

Chapter Fifteen

Thea tried to suppress a vicious smile. It was a fitting punishment and far more justice than she had thought they would get. It was going to be hard to not take an inordinate amount of pleasure in it. She slid a sideways glance at the other women. They were watching Barik with a strange gleam in their eyes. They smiled queerly as they watched him writhe on the floor.

She looked behind her at Kyrin and Daeshen. They, too, watched Barik twist and shake with dark pleasure. Her own feeling of satisfaction faded. It was sad. Even the punishment was sad. She knew she shouldn't take pleasure in another's pain. It made her no better than him. "Lady?" she whispered hesitantly. "Lord?"

The God and Goddess turned and looked at her enquiringly. They glided toward her with steps so smooth it was as if they didn't need to use any muscles. It was disconcerting to watch.

She looked down at the floor and switched to English. "I don't want to be the person who takes pleasure in another's misfortune." She looked up at them solemnly. "It would be really easy for me to do the happy dance right now and I know I shouldn't."

Gaia rolled her eyes. "Quit trying to be perfect, Thea. It's irritating," she replied, also in English.

Thea glowered at the floor. "I'm not trying to be perfect!"

Gaia snorted. "You're trying, all right. You just haven't made it. You'd have to quit throwing books at your husbands first."

Thea blushed bright red. *Damn.*

"There is darkness in all things, child, even Us," Skye stated quietly. "But there is something you could do to lessen the sorrow of his family," he continued, watching Barik's mother. She looked near collapse.

"What's that?" Thea asked warily. She had a feeling she should have kept her mouth shut.

"She has lost both her children," he replied, waving an arm toward her. "You could give her another."

Thea felt the blood drain from her face. She swayed on her feet. She was barely aware of Kyrin and Daeshen standing and quickly coming to her side. "What?" she asked, her voice hoarse with disbelief.

Skye sighed softly. "It is a hard thing We ask. I know this, daughter."

Thea let out a choked laugh that held no humor. "Hard?" She looked around. The court asana and High Queen were watching them curiously, but without recognition. Thea realized they were still speaking in English. "Her family has already produced a suicide and a rapist. You want me to give them another chance?" She shook her head slowly.

Gaia frowned down at her sternly. "Just as a child is not responsible for the actions of their parents, so too are their parents not always responsible for their children's actions. For shame, daughter. She would do anything to change what has happened!"

Thea hung her head. She knew that, but what They asked... She didn't know if she could do it.

Kyrin and Daeshen moved protectively closer.

"What do They want, Thea?" Kyrin asked cautiously. He, too, spoke in English, understanding this conversation was to be kept private.

"They want me to carry a child for Barik's parents," she whispered.

He stiffened against her. She waited for the explosion.

It didn't come. She looked up at her husband. She watched the struggle on his face as he visibly tried to relax his muscles. Then, she looked at Daeshen, who was shaking his head slowly in disbelief.

"Their son killed our child!" he finally burst out.

The room went silent and everyone turned to stare. Those who could understand English began to whisper amongst themselves.

Thea stroked his arm. "I will not carry Barik's child," she stated quietly, but firmly. Both men relaxed beside her.

Behind Gaia and Skye, the Lithen of the Ta'e'sha coalesced.

All the Ta'e'sha in the room rose again and knelt in the presence of their Gods.

Samonan approached the trio anxiously. "There is a way, niece. We could help." Her hands twisted together.

Thea looked up at the sad Goddess. "How?" she asked tiredly. "I could not bear to carry his child. I-I think my body would abort it." She shook her head.

Kysout moved to stand next to his mate with a flick of his tail. Behind them, the remaining eight Gods and Goddess watched hopefully. Kysout moved his hand in a complicated motion. A pale, yellow-green light appeared. It formed into a small Ta'e'shian woman with spring green hair and tail. Her eyes shone like peridot jewels.

"B-b-balai?" Barik's mother choked out, reaching toward the woman.

Balai turned and smiled gently at her mother. She turned back to Thea and watched her without saying anything.

Samonan motioned toward Balai. "You could carry her child."

Behind them Barik screamed and threw himself toward his sister. "*No!* No, no, no! Don't touch my sister!" The guards jumped on him and quickly wrestled him to the floor. He thrashed desperately under them, his ravaged face etched with grief and hatred. His fingernails cracked and tore as he tried to crawl toward them. Howls filled the air, making the people watching shudder in reaction.

Balai watched sadly. Thea could see that the ghost loved her brother and mourned what had happened to him. She moved through the air to where Claudette, Sarah, Joyce, and Giana stood watching. "I am so sorry," she whispered in a voice that faded as soon as it met the air. Next, she swayed to Barik and looked down at him, her face a mask of sorrow. "You are lost to me now, brother."

He keened loudly as she left him, his mind completely broken.

Balai blew a kiss to her mother and father. "I love you; tell all my parents." Her mother sobbed and watched her with hungry eyes.

Kysout sighed softly. "Come back, Balai."

She returned to her original position and watched Thea again.

Thea looked down at the floor. "How? She is dead." Kyrin and Daeshen tensed beside her again. She looked back up.

All the Gods and Goddesses of Ta'e held up their hands. Colors began to swirl at Balai's abdomen. A small ball of light detached itself and floated up to Thea's eye level. It spun for a moment before turning into a glass globe the color of Balai's eyes. A tiny pinpoint of light glowed within.

"Just keep this globe safe, and should you decide to do this for Us, hold it to your stomach. The child will be conceived. The pregnancy will be easy and quick. Please, think on it, niece," Samonan said softly.

The Lithen and Balai faded away. Thea took the globe from the air and stared at it.

Gaia and Skye each kissed her forehead.

"The decision is yours, daughter. Should you decide not to do this, few will know," Gaia said softly.

The Ta'e'sha rose again as Gaia and Skye popped out with a flash of light.

The High Queen returned to her seat. She motioned to the aide standing behind her and whispered in his ear. He nodded.

The guards pulled Barik to his feet and dragged him out a side door.

Shayateen addressed the room. "Barik shall be placed in the custody of the Temples. Visitors will be allowed only with written permission by my office." She motioned to Thea. "Theadora, please come here."

Thea gulped and walked slowly to the table, still carefully holding the globe. "Yes, my lady?"

The High Queen studied her silently for a moment. "Well, you have certainly treated the court to many things we have never seen before," she said at length. "Would you care to enlighten us to the conversation that brought our Lithen to you? And the meaning of that object you are holding so carefully, as well, please."

Thea stroked her thumb over the globe. "They would like me to carry Balai's child and give it to her mother to raise," she said softly.

The asana leaned toward her to hear her better.

"This globe contains that child's life force." She met the queen's gaze squarely. "I don't know what I'll do yet. I have to talk to my husbands and fiancée."

The queen leaned back in her chair. "I do not know this word, fiancée."

"It means betrothed, Your Majesty."

"I see. Where is your betrothed?"

"She was not given permission to attend, Your Majesty. So, she went home to visit her family," Thea said quietly.

The High Queen tapped her nails on the table for several minutes. Finally she said, "I do not want to influence your decision, but I would like to point out that Karenina's line will die out when she passes. The power of her Royal line will go to a cousin, also sterile and without a fertile daughter." Karenina was Barik's mother. "I would not like to see her line die." The queen looked at her steadily.

Thea thought quickly. She slowly raised her eyebrow. "Is that a Royal decree?" she finally asked in a cold tone. *Not influence my decision, my ass!*

The queen looked startled.

Thea didn't back down.

"A Royal decree? It is not." Shayateen's face hardened. "It is a strong suggestion."

Thea felt her Irish temper begin to smolder. She stomped to the evidence table and snatched up the casket containing her child's body. She strode back and carefully set it on the table before the queen. "Your people have taken much from me," she said in a low, carefully controlled voice. "I have no roots here. I have no family, other than those of my husbands. I have survived being attacked by a madman. I survived the death of my child. What I do have is the love of my God and Goddess, the love of my husbands and fiancée. I have my body and I *will* have my choice." She pointed at the casket. "That baby died because someone else thought I was the cause of his problems. Your asana wanted to do tests on those fragile tissues to see if it was a boy or girl. I refused to let them touch my child. It should not matter. Would Barik have been tried more harshly if it were a girl? It was a baby. It was a life. That's all that should matter." She took a deep breath. "What gives you the right to ask this of me? You don't know me. I doubt you have more than a passing care for me. Are you friends with Karenina? Is that why you think you should make this decision for me? That you can disregard how I would feel?" She set the globe beside the casket and pointed at it. "That little glowing light is related to the man who extinguished that glowing little light." She moved her hand to point at the casket.

"Would you like it if someone ordered you to carry the niece or nephew of the man who killed your child in your body? Would you caress your stomach? Would you love it? Or would you feel you had betrayed your child's memory?" She placed her hands on the table and leaned forward, ignoring the nervous twitches of the Warrior Chosen guards behind the queen. "I will make this decision. Not you. I will discuss it with my husbands. Not you. I have only one queen and you just met her."

The High Queen stared at Thea in shock. She rapidly had to reassess her estimation of the small, dark-haired woman standing before her. During the trial she had come to the conclusion Thea was fragile and easily swayed. Obviously, the woman who had trembled and hid her face during the viewing of the attack had many layers to her, and, perhaps, they hid a core of pure tempered steel. She slid a glance at Thea's husbands. Kyrin was staring at his wife with slack-jawed shock while Daeshen just looked resigned. She thought she detected a faint gleam of amusement in his eyes.

Not since she had been a child had someone dared to speak to her that way. It was not pleasant and she had to acknowledge she had, indeed, overstepped her bounds. She had forgotten the women of Earth were not her subjects. She sent a message to her aides on a mental thread. "*We must address the situation of the Earth women's citizenship tomorrow.*"

She thought about what Thea had said to her. She would never have tried to apply pressure to a Ta'e'shian woman like that. She was guilty of the very thing her God and Goddess had warned her about.

She unconsciously thought of the human women as less.

It would have to stop. Beginning with her. Personal feelings had no place in ruling a planet, but they did intrude. Somehow, she would have to find a way to change her perception.

But, for now, she had to hold herself accountable for her own actions.

"You are correct, Theadora Auralel. It is not my place to force a decision on you. I apologize," she said slowly. The conversation had been kept low so the gallery could not hear them.

There was a collective indrawn breath from the asana seated around her. She knew what they were thinking. The queen did not apologize. The queen's word was absolute.

She had watched the recordings of the visit her Gods had first made in Thea's bedroom and perhaps the asana were not the only ones who had let their station elevate their sense of self worth. She, more than most, had to realize that being queen was for her people. Not for her.

Thea nodded her acceptance of the apology. "I apologize for my outburst. I think everyone's emotions are running high today. This has been a trying situation."

Shayateen smiled. The human woman was gracious, more gracious than many would have been in the same situation. She leaned forward and placed her hand on Thea's. "I would like to know you better. Would you and your husbands join my family for dinner this evening?"

Thea turned to look at her husbands. They nodded their acceptance. She turned back to the queen. "That would be lovely."

"Excellent," Shayateen said with satisfaction. "My aide will contact you with the time." She sent a signal to her aide, who quickly came forward and announced the end of the trial and court. She stood and left the courtroom.

Thea turned back to her husbands. "Daeshen? Could you speak with the queen's aide?"

He nodded.

She picked up the globe and then the casket. "May I take my child home now?" she asked the remaining asana.

The High Priestess of the Balance Temple nodded gently. "We would not have been harsher if you had lost a daughter, Theadora," she said quietly.

Thea looked at the floor. "It's just very hard for me, ma'am." When she looked back up, the priestess was preparing to leave. The lady nodded to Thea and left with the rest of the asana.

Thea turned around and almost ran into Kyrin. He took the tiny casket from her and stroked her cheek with his free hand. "Are you ready to leave, love?" he asked her.

She shook her head. "Almost." She slid around him and nervously approached Barik's mother, Karenina. The woman's husband was trying to pull her from her chair, unsuccessfully. He glared halfheartedly at Thea but did not speak.

Thea knelt before the shattered woman and took her hand.

Karenina looked at her dazedly. Her hand was limp in Thea's and her hair had fallen lifelessly around her.

Thea took a deep breath and opened herself to the other woman's pain. It was staggering. Sharp spears of agony radiated from her heart. "It wasn't your fault. None of it was." She drew the pain slowly away.

Karenina's eyes slowly focused on Thea's face. "How can you know that? Both my children are gone. That is not the son I raised."

Thea caressed her face gently and ignored the faint growling noises Karenina's husband was making. She could feel the anguish lessening and saw the results in the woman's breathing, which was easier. "Remember him as he was before. Not as he is now."

"What did my daughter say to you?" she asked Thea hoarsely.

Thea sighed and looked down. "It is not for me to say yet." She patted Karenina's hand. "Just remember what she said to *you.*"

Karenina smiled wanly. "I will." She touched the globe with a hesitant finger. "That is the color of her eyes. She had such beautiful eyes. Her laugh was as warm as sunshine. My baby girl brought joy to everyone."

Thea held out the globe. "Would you like to hold it?"

The other woman nodded and took the globe gently. "It reminds me of her." She cradled it gently in her palms. Her husband knelt beside Thea and gently touched a finger to it.

He looked at Thea sideways. "I know what this is. I absorbed the English language when we were notified of what happened," he said softly in English. He was referring to the subliminal lessons the Ta'e'sha used to learn languages while they were asleep. "Please do not say anything to my wife if you decide to refuse."

Thea looked at him in surprise. "I will not," she replied softly, also in English. "I can't decide right now though. It's too fresh."

He nodded. "I understand."

Karenina gave Thea back the globe and squeezed her hand. "Thank you for talking to me. Thank you for not hating me."

Thea closed off the part of herself that was empathic and stood. "It was a pleasure. May I call on your family before we leave town?"

Karenina nodded. "I would like that."

* * *

Thea stared at the wall. She needed some time to herself, so she had sent the guys off to get some dinner to bring back to the room. Last night had been strained; she wasn't used to eating dinner with a queen. Hopefully she didn't offend anyone too badly. She really needed to brush up on Ta'e'shian dining etiquette. On the plus side, the queen was much friendlier than Thea had expected and had asked a great many questions about Earth and her cultures. It was her hope the queen would begin to see humans in a better light. But only time would tell.

The princess was very shy and had barely spoken through most of the meal. She would ask a few questions and then seem to draw into herself to absorb the answers. It was somewhat disconcerting.

The Royal Consorts, Bashar and Shaaden, had been more interested in the animals of Earth. Daeshen had gotten along with them very well, since biology was one of his favorite subjects.

Although Thea now knew more about the physiology of naked mole rats than she had ever wanted to know. The queen had seemed quietly amused by the whole conversation.

A thump in the hall brought her attention back to the present. A few moments passed and Thea decided it wasn't her husbands returning. She glanced over at the green globe sitting on the dresser. She had placed a small pillow under it to keep it from rolling off. The small glowing light inside seemed to move closer to the side of the globe. Thea had the impression it was looking out at her. It shimmered gently and spun in circles before returning to the side of the globe again.

Thea smiled sadly. It was alive. She could feel it in her heart. Every time she looked at it, she felt like it was looking back out at her. She made a mental note to cover it up when she had sex with her husbands.

The door handle jiggled for a moment and then the door opened. Daeshen and Kyrin marched in wearing identical smirks. *Uh oh*, she thought to herself. "What's for dinner?" she asked, ignoring the evil gleams being bestowed upon her.

"You," Kyrin replied with a rakish grin.

"That doesn't sound very filling," Thea countered dryly.

"The filling part is our job," Daeshen said with a leer.

Thea had to laugh at that.

Kyrin dropped a few bags and started digging through them. Thea watched curiously. *It's a good thing I'm not starving*, she thought to herself. It looked like dinner had been postponed.

Kyrin pulled something out a bag and held it up to her with a flourish. It looked like a bodysuit made out of wire.

She stared at it blankly.

The men stared at it like kids in a candy store.

A minute passed.

"Okay, I give up. What is it?" she finally asked.

"It's a Sparker," Daeshen said in a reverent tone.

"What's a Sparker?"

"We'll show you, my beauty," Kyrin replied, drawing her out of her chair. He began unbuttoning her shirt.

"Umm, babe?" Thea wasn't sure about wearing a pair of wire underwear with a name that implied electricity. She batted at Kyrin's hands as he started tugging at her pants. "Guys?"

They just grinned at her.

Her muscles started twitching when they didn't answer her. She grabbed Kyrin's wrists and shook her head nervously. "No, Kyrin, stop, I don't want to."

He stilled and met her gaze. She trembled. "It's okay, love. Trust us; you know we won't hurt you." He cupped her face, her hands still circling his wrists. "You trusted us once. Trust us again; don't let him take that from us." He pressed a gentle kiss against her lips.

Thea sighed into his mouth and her eyes fluttered closed. He was right, she had trusted them, but now she couldn't stand them dominating her. She couldn't tolerate feeling helpless. Her mouth tingled where his lips feathered soft kisses across it.

She broke the kiss and met his soulful gaze again. She saw the awareness in it. He knew what he was asking of her. If she said no they would respect that, but at what cost? She had missed the delicious sensations of their hands bringing her those painful pleasures she craved. They had missed them as well. But, even more, they had missed the casual touches and being able to enjoy making love without having to think about and weigh the consequences of their every action.

She slowly released his hands and smiled tremulously. "I'll try."

A tear slid down Kyrin's cheek. He drew in a shuddering breath. "Thank you, love. You are everything to us."

She stood on tiptoe and kissed him tenderly. She had never meant to hurt them.

Daeshen came forward, his face solemn. "If it's too much just tell us to stop, Thea."

She looked up at him. He rarely used her name; instead, he almost always called her darling. It told her how very serious he was. She gave him a wobbly smile. "I will."

They carefully removed her clothing. Holding Daeshen's hand for balance, she carefully stepped into the suit. It fit her perfectly. She had no idea how her husbands had managed it.

Kyrin went to his knees before her and gently spread her thighs. She gripped Daeshen's hand tighter and placed her feet about three feet apart. Kyrin's fingers brushed her soft, hairless mound. She hadn't noticed that the crotch of the suit was split open until he began to clip the edges to the rings piercing her labia.

He paused to nibble on her soft flesh. Thea moaned in reaction, tipping her hips into the caress. After a last lingering lick, he fastened the final clip. He reached up and adjusted the wires circling her nipples. That finished, he stood and smiled down at her.

Daeshen spread his fingers under her hair and tapped the wires gently.

The suit began to shrink around her. It stopped just short of pain. She looked down and her skin puffed between the latticework of wires. Blood flowed into the constricted areas making her skin more sensitive.

Daeshen reached into another bag and drew out a wide black velvet ribbon. Watching her face, he slowly wound it around one of her wrists, then the other. When she didn't protest, he finished winding the length around both wrists and tied the ends into a pretty bow.

Thea trembled, and she knew she was watching them with huge, nervous eyes. Kyrin's hands skimmed over the skin puffed out by the suit. It was an amazing sensation; her nerves jumped and sang as the blood-engorged skin was stimulated. "Oh," she murmured softly, "that feels nice."

Daeshen moved behind her and rubbed her ass slowly. His lips feathered across her shoulder and up her neck. She quivered when his teeth nipped her ear. "I want you here tonight," he whispered sensually into the shell of her ear. His fingers slid between her cheeks and rubbed the rose of her anus.

Thea shivered before relaxing into the caress. They had never taken her there. She was nervous about it. They had prepared her for it with toys. Smaller toys. Daeshen would stretch her painfully, and she realized she wanted that.

Both men stepped away from her and undressed each other. Smooth skin was slowly exposed with each dropped piece of fabric. Their bodies moved closer together as the last pieces fell.

There was so much love in their eyes as they trailed caresses along the other's body. She loved watching them together and never felt like she meant less to them. It was times like this that she felt the ties binding them together and knew she had made the right decision by staying with them and trying to build a life together.

Kyrin cupped Daeshen's face and pressed a deep, openmouthed kiss onto his lips. Their erect penises brushed and then were hidden from view as their bodies fused together. Kyrin's arm twisted around Daeshen's slim waist and he hauled the smaller man ever tighter against him.

Thea toyed with her nipples as she watched them. Daeshen's tongue flicked out to tickle the top of Kyrin's lips. It wasn't often she just got to watch; they always dragged her into their play. She sat back on the chair, hooked her legs over the arms, and caressed the dampening flesh between her thighs. The velvet ribbon tickled her thighs; she moved her hands so that her sweet spot was hidden by the bow.

The kiss slowly broke off and both men turned to look at her. Cheek to cheek they stroked each other's bodies as they watched Thea press a finger into her sheath and slowly stroke in and out. She smiled at them and drew the finger out and delicately licked her fluids off it.

Kyrin moved to stand behind Daeshen. He cupped the heavy weight of Daeshen's jewels and caressed the hard stalk of his erection. Daeshen's head fell back onto Kyrin's shoulder and he moaned softly.

"Do you want him?" Kyrin asked in a harsh whisper.

Thea spread her lower lips and trailed a fingertip around her clit. "Yes," she replied in a hushed voice.

Kyrin set his teeth into the curve of Daeshen's shoulder and bit down slowly.

Daeshen shuddered.

Thea trembled, wanting those teeth on her. She wanted the mark that appeared as those strong white teeth scraped free, leaving a blooming pink. She licked her lips, watching them hungrily. Blood pooled in her breasts, engorging her nipples further. Heat pooled low in her belly and her sheath pulsed with empty aches.

"He was mine first," Kyrin murmured, turning Daeshen to the side and moving in front of him again. "Maybe I don't want to share tonight." He bent his head and lapped Daeshen's nipples, pulling his head back with a firm grip in his hair.

Daeshen purred, curving his hands around Kyrin's arms. Thea whimpered, watching their bodies sway against each other teasingly.

Kyrin turned his head and watched Thea from the corner of his eye as he bit Daeshen's throat and suckled the smooth flesh.

Thea whimpered, her fingers stroking faster.

Kyrin slid down Daeshen's body and took that heavy stem into his mouth. Thea watched, mesmerized, as he slowly drew the entire length in. It filled his throat for a moment before he slowly drew away. The head popped free with a wet sound. Kyrin rested his cheek against it as he watched Thea toy with her aching core. "Perhaps I'll take him tonight, over and over again, until there is nothing left for you." He turned his head a fraction of an inch and lapped Daeshen's cock.

Thea's gaze flew to Daeshen's face. His head rolled lazily on his shoulders. He gave her a smoky, heavy-lidded smile. She was not reassured. *They won't really leave me,* she whispered to herself. *Will they?*

Kyrin's hair curled around Daeshen's throbbing rod. It netted around him and pulsed, constricting and releasing him slowly as Kyrin's tongue fluttered across and around the crown.

Thea licked her lips again as a pearly drop of precum trembled on the tip. She moaned with disappointment when Kyrin's tongue caught it and drew it into his mouth.

He smiled darkly at Thea and hummed with pleasure. "He's so delicious, lover. Do you want some?"

She nodded, feeling dazed. Only they could cloud her mind with desire so quickly. She had never felt like this about anyone else. When she had lived on Earth, she had wondered if there was something wrong with her. The men hadn't sent a single pulse of lust through her. Now, here she was, trembling with want, aching for them.

She wished Sya'tia were here to see this. They could make the men shake like aspen leaves in the wind. She vowed that when they reached Sya'tia's home that she would return the favor.

Thinking about her beautiful fiancée made the ache inside her strengthen. She cried out, pressing two fingers inside her to ease the burn.

Daeshen growled, watching her.

She smiled seductively, arching her back so her breasts pressed even tighter against the wires decorating her.

Suddenly, the wires began to vibrate and send delicate shocks through her breasts and nether lips. She arched against the chair in surprise and writhed.

Through glazed eyes she watched her husbands smile darkly.

"Enough of that, you," Kyrin said, still lapping the head of Daeshen's cock. "Bad girl, teasing your husbands like that."

"Bad girls should get spankings," Daeshen murmured in a thick voice. "Hard, hot, fast spankings."

Thea's breath caught in her throat at his words, but she couldn't reply because that devilish suit continued to torment her with delicious sparks and tingles.

Kyrin swiped a final taste and stood. "I think you are right, my heart."

They advanced on her with leisurely steps. She knew they were enjoying the view of her twisting and shivering in the chair while her fingers moved quickly in and out of her sex.

Daeshen drew her out of the chair by grasping her bound wrists and pulling her fingers free.

Kyrin approached, holding another ribbon she hadn't seen him get. He lifted it toward her face.

Thea realized he was going to bind her eyes and she drew back nervously.

Kyrin smiled tenderly in response. "Trust," he whispered.

She nodded, her knees weak from desire. The fear was a sumptuous velvet wave inside her. She hoped she wouldn't panic, but they were being so very careful with her that it gave her hope.

The velvet slid around her eyes, and darkness fell. She felt him tie the ends behind her head and stood trembling as the wires heated and vibrated faster. Harsh gasps escaped her throat as Daeshen pulled her across the room, patient with her hesitant steps.

Kyrin walked quietly behind the two of them. He and Daeshen had melded their thoughts together so they could better monitor Thea. She was feeling apprehensive, but the desire overrode the tension. He knew she wanted this and was trying to work through her fear.

He loved teasing her and wondered why they hadn't done it before. "*We should tie her up and make her watch us make love next time. Perhaps even take Sya'tia and leave Thea aching for us...*" he whispered in Daeshen's mind.

"*Oh yes,*" was the soft reply.

They helped Thea onto the bed and pressed her shoulders so she knelt on the soft coverlet. Her bound hands were under her and they positioned her so her shoulders and upper chest were resting against the soft fabric.

Each man took a position kneeling beside her; their hands rubbed and caressed her bound form. Their thoughts were so closely entwined they felt like one mind in two bodies. They had never tried this before but the sensations were wonderful.

Daeshen's hand slipped under her and he pinched her nipple hard. She gasped and jerked. Both men sighed at the honey-sweet pain flowed from her like wine -- warm, sweet, and just as intoxicating. His other hand traveled over her ass and slid a finger hard into her weeping sheath. Warm liquid flowed down her thighs.

Kyrin growled low in his throat as he felt her twitching muscles welcome the intruder through their link. His hand crashed down on her upturned ass in a stinging blow.

They all shuddered at the impact.

Daeshen pulled his fingers free and trailed them between her ass cheeks. He moistened the tight rose there.

Kyrin slapped his hand down again. Pink bloomed between the white lines created by the constricting wires. He watched Daeshen collect more nectar from Thea's core and return to massage it into the tight hole he coveted. He twisted slightly to the side and snagged the bottle of lube they kept on the bedside table to toss it to Daeshen, who caught it and set it by his knee.

She whimpered under them uncertainly. They reacted to the fear beginning to overtake her with soft kisses along her back. She gentled again only to tense as Daeshen's finger began to slowly, surely penetrate her.

Both men hummed with pleasure as the finger seated itself to the knuckle. Kyrin began to lay systematic slaps on her ass around his husband's wrist as Daeshen leaned down to bite Thea's shoulder. "We are going to fuck you all night long, little one." His teeth bit down hard again. "Over and over and over until you are screaming, and then we will fuck you again." The bite turned deep red, Kyrin noted with satisfaction. It would leave a pretty bruise.

Her knees slid down, dislodging Daeshen's finger. Kyrin quickly slapped her thigh. "Up, now."

She quickly slid back into position as he continued to slap and pinch her thighs. Soft moans escaped her lips. He pressed her legs apart and landed a slap on her bare, wet pussy.

She jerked and cried out.

Daeshen bit her again as Kyrin focused his stinging blows on the slippery mound between her legs. He smiled as she jerked and writhed after each slap. More juice oozed, wetting his hand.

Daeshen released her and moved to kneel behind their beloved. Kyrin rubbed her, and he watched with satisfaction as his husband dipped his fingers into the slick liquid and coated his purpling shaft. It took several teasing dips before he was coated thoroughly and glistening in the dimming light of the room.

Kyrin slipped up to Thea's head and bunched her hair in his hand. He lifted her head and brushed his cock against her open mouth. "Suck." He slid inside and she began to draw him in eagerly.

Daeshen parted her ass cheeks. He squeezed a bit of the lube onto her rose and then set the tip of his cock between them. Thea tensed under them but didn't protest, so he began to slowly penetrate her, taking his time.

She whimpered around Kyrin's cock, and he sent small pulses of desire and love to her until she relaxed again. Still, he removed his cock from her mouth and bent down to spread soft kisses across her lips and cheeks.

She gasped, her mouth blindly seeking his.

He felt her jerk and tremble and knew from that and the dark satisfaction radiating from Daeshen that he was seated firmly inside her. There was something about Thea that made them both want to beat their chests and roar.

He lifted back onto his knees and filled her seeking mouth with his swollen member. With easy, gentle thrusts he began to fuck her mouth while Daeshen rocked against Thea's rosy red ass.

He blended his mind back with Daeshen's and enjoyed the tight warmth superimposed over his cock. It was as if he fucking her in both places at the same time. He shivered as her teeth grazed his sensitive penis.

The sweet pain rolling off Thea added another layer to their pleasure, and he shared it all with her. Her teeth bit down slightly in reaction and she jerked. After a moment she relaxed and moaned deep in her throat; he responded by pushing himself farther in and withdrawing just before she choked.

Using his cerebcom he upped the voltage coursing through the wires and grinned when both she and Daeshen jerked and moaned.

He admired Daeshen's cock sliding easily in and out of the stretched opening of his wife's body. It was delicious.

Suddenly a dark cloud of fear and helplessness stopped all three of them. Thea thrashed under them and they quickly held her. Kyrin withdrew from her gasping mouth and he whispered softly in her ear. They had feared this.

Daeshen stroked her hips and back, sending love and reassurances to her.

She stilled and trembled, listening to them. "Kyrin?" she whispered in a shattered voice.

"We're here, love, you're safe," he murmured softly against her hair.

"Okay, okay," she panted out. Her arms slid under her and she lifted onto her elbows but didn't pull away from Daeshen. "Can you take off the blindfold?" she asked, her voice shaking.

Kyrin quickly tugged it free and cupped her cheeks.

She blinked a few times before her eyes focused on his a bit desperately. He felt the panic recede.

"Better?"

She nodded against his hands and relaxed again.

He "felt" Daeshen twitch inside her and she moaned softly, her passion rising again. Her mouth opened and she licked his straining erection. He placed it against her lips again and she drew him deeply in.

He caressed her cheeks and began to move again, thrusting gently in and out. Daeshen smiled and began to move as well. His hands curved around her ultrasensitive hips and cradled her against his pelvis.

Reaching down, Kyrin cupped her firm breasts, held tightly in the wire suit, and rubbed his palms against her nipples. She sighed and lifted better into his hands as she jolted in time to Daeshen's increasingly urgent thrusts.

Kyrin shuddered when she moaned around his cock again. He felt more than saw Daeshen's hand cup her wet mound and slip two fingers into her lonely pussy. Daeshen's palm rubbed her clit with each quick thrust of his fingers.

Thea made soft mewling noises around his cock as Daeshen began to slam harder against her ass. Small jolts of burning pain echoed along their link each time his pelvis slammed into her paddled cheeks.

Suddenly both of his mates screamed and shuddered. Kyrin jerked as their orgasms rocked through him. He gritted his teeth to keep from joining them.

Thea twisted and shook under them while Daeshen held her tightly to him, trembling ecstatically.

They both sagged and panted, his cock slipped from her mouth. He released the pressure on the suit and watched, lazily curling his fingers around his prick and stroking it slowly.

After a few minutes Daeshen finished coming and withdrew tiredly. He lay down on his side and smile beatifically.

Kyrin sat back and stretched out one leg and bent the other at the knee.

Thea stirred and lifted up. She smiled and started to slip off the bed.

Kyrin's hand shot out and grabbed the back of her neck, making her jump. "Where do you think you're going?" He pulled her face back to his throbbing dick. "You're not done yet." He smiled with pleasure as her mouth opened submissively and she began to suck him again.

Immediately her desire bloomed again and he enjoyed every moment of it. Leaning back, he relaxed and rubbed her scalp as she pleasured him. They wouldn't stop until their wife was their perfect sex slave again.

Daeshen had been right: they were going to fuck her all night. Over and over again. Until she wanted to be their slave just as much.

* * *

Aboard the Dark Queen

Gaia shimmered into being in an empty cabin. She opened her mouth and a clear bell-like tone echoed through the air. While she waited, a soft voice floated through her head.

"Thank you for helping My daughters, Sister. I worried your daughter would turn them from Me, but that is not her way, is it?" A breeze touched her cheek for a moment. It felt like a kiss. She smiled and sent back a pulse of affection to that nameless voice.

For all that the Gods and Goddesses bickered and insulted each other, They were siblings and loved each other as such. Their charges rarely understood that.

She continued to wait patiently for Her children to come to her.

One by one they began to trickle into the room.

When the last member of her merry band of mischief makers appeared, she sat down. They formed a semicircle around her. The cats sat back on their haunches and watched her expectantly, and the birds shook their feathers to sit on the floor near their cat companions.

"Excellent work, My darlings. I think the Ta'e'sha would kill you if they caught you," she said with a smirk. "You can stop now. I believe I have finally gotten the message across to them and My brothers and sisters. What would you like to do now? You may stay and take up a life with your charges or you may pass on."

She waited patiently as she listened to the mental conversations going on around her. It only took a few minutes for them to come to a decision.

Condezl stood and stretched out a cat bow to Gaia. "Lady, we cats would like to stay with our ladies. We would like to show ourselves to them and be their friends." His mouth dropped open in a feline grin. "After all, every witch needs a familiar!"

Gaia laughed softy. "So be it." She looked enquiringly at Myst.

Myst stood and hopped forward to bob a bow. "My Lady, we birds would like to wait until the new Earth is terraformed. Then we would like to go to it and give our lore to the animals that will live there. Many will not know their history, and we would like to give it to them."

Gaia smiled happily. "Oh, My children, I am pleased! I shall take your requests for transplant to the Great One. My beautiful kittens, you shall stay here until your ladies return. I wish you a joyous incarnation."

She stood and hugged each of the cats. "Should you need Me, just call!" With that, she gathered the birds to her and they all faded slowly from view.

Condezl looked around. "Well, let's go check out our new digs! I am so going to ask Thea to make me a high-walled bed out of raw silk!" He purred with anticipated pleasure.

The other cats growled and purred in agreement, and then they parted ways to inspect their new homes.

Condezl paused when he heard the Lady's voice in his head. "I do not wish Barik to die, child. Leave him to his torment and wish him a long and healthy life. Be at peace; she has been avenged." He sighed to himself. He would do as his Lady commanded.

Chapter Sixteen

Thea rubbed her back as she slinked out of the vehicle. It had been yet another long and tedious journey. They had left the capital city early that morning, and it was quickly approaching dark now.

Still rubbing her back, she looked around. They were parked in a large paved lot overlooking a huge cove neatly encircled by black rock cliffs broken by a large vee of stone and rock that led to the open ocean. The placid blue waters looked cool and inviting. She was looking forward to swimming later. Hopefully, this would be a relaxing stay.

She sighed with pleasure when Kyrin came up behind her and rubbed her lower back. A dull ache had developed there early in the trip and hadn't gone away in spite of the low dose of painkiller she had taken. She wondered if she was going to start her menstrual cycle soon. Her cycles had been very irregular since the miscarriage, but Corvin didn't seem worried about it. He had advised her to wait and let her body settle into a rhythm on its own.

Corvin stopped next to her and looked around curiously. He had decided to come with them because Sya'tia had called last night to ask him if her sisters could have two of the eggs she had allowed to be harvested in past months.

The remaining fertile women had been asked to allow doctors to harvest their eggs if they were not actively trying to have children. Thea had discovered it was a painful process and she had great respect for the women taking part. She had watched Sya'tia take shots and vitamins every day before an egg was harvested. Eggs were not taken from the women every cycle, as the strain would be too great for their bodies. Usually, they rested for four or five months before donating again.

She had asked Corvin about the actual procedure to remove the egg, and it still made her turn green to think about it. She was just grateful she didn't have to do it. Her eggs could only be fertilized by her husbands, since their DNA was what was used to convert her body so she could carry their children.

Her thoughts were interrupted by a short lady with brown hair approaching with fast mincing steps. She was wearing a robe that reminded Thea of a Japanese kimono. The lady had a broad smile across her face and waved her hands anxiously.

"Hello, hello, hello! You must be the Auralels!" She stopped in front of them and began passing out hugs and kisses like they were Halloween candy.

Thea laughed and returned the hug and kiss. "I'm Thea. These are my husbands, Daeshen and Kyrin. And our friend, Corvin."

The woman beamed. "I am Kokia, Sya'tia's mother. I'm so glad you could come! She should be here soon; she's swimming back from the fields." She waved her hand toward the blue expanse of water. "Most of our houses are in the rock of the cove, but we keep this one for visitors. Oh, there she is now." Kokia shaded her eyes and stared intently at the water.

Sya'tia came flying out of the water before diving below again. Water sparkled like jewels on her snowy scales. Thea caught her breath as Sya'tia continued to jump like a dolphin, quickly closing the gap between her and the shore. It was a magical sight. She was so graceful and sure of herself in the water that Thea could only marvel. The pools on the ship didn't allow Sya'tia to reach her full range of speed, and this was the first time Thea had seen her swim so fast.

The strength granted to her by being born Warrior Chosen was evident in every muscular flex of her body and the sheer amount of water she cleared with each leap. It took her only moments to reach the shore and change to her human form.

Completely unself-conscious about her partial nudity, she ran to them and kissed them exuberantly. Thea heard a faint approving hum from Corvin as he admired Sya'tia's firm body when she returned the hug and kiss bestowed upon her. "I've missed you!" She had her marriage veil tied around her waist; it was the only clothing she was wearing. Her strong body glimmered in the late evening sun.

Corvin stepped forward to take her hands and pressed a kiss on Sya'tia's cheek. He sighed theatrically. "If only all my patients were in as good shape as you, my dear. It's a joy to watch you move, as always."

Sya'tia giggled softly. She grabbed several of the cases their driver had taken out of the vehicle. "C'mon, I'll show you the house. Mother, could you make tea?"

Kokia nodded, her bright eyes still busily inspecting them. Thea winked, making the woman laugh as they followed Sya'tia.

They were given a room decorated in purples and golds. It reminded Thea of a movie producer's idea of what a harem would look like. Huge pillows were strewn about the floor in a deceptively casual way. The bed had a canopy draped with contrasting swathes of fabric while the bed itself looked like it had been created by layering huge futons on top of each other. She loved seeing all the different styles of décor she had been introduced to since they landed.

Sya'tia disappeared with Corvin to show him to another room. She was chattering a mile a minute at him as they left. Her voice trailed off as they moved down the hall.

Thea turned and pounced on Kyrin. She wrapped her legs around his waist and clung to his neck to give him a lingering kiss. His arms curled under her legs to support her weight as he returned the kiss with interest.

He sighed happily when the kiss ended. "What was that for?" he asked her, his eyes heavy lidded with pleasure.

Thea beamed. "I'm just happy. The trial's over and Chisha is coming around." She leaned closer to whisper in his ear, "I think we should get her laid."

Daeshen laughed behind them. "I heard that!" He came to them and bent forward to nip Thea's earlobe.

She giggled, leaning against Kyrin's arms to kiss her other husband. "You never know, it might help!"

Sya'tia cleared her throat from the doorway. Thea peeked over Kyrin's shoulder to smile at her. She had obviously stopped to put on some clothes before coming back to them. She was wearing a sapphire blue halter top and matching shorts made of a wispy floating fabric. The colors glowed against her pale skin and Thea admired the design. Not every woman looked good in a halter top, but it framed Sya'tia's muscular shoulders to perfection. The shorts made her legs look a mile long and model sleek. She had twisted her hair into multiple braids and was wearing her veil like a headband with the remaining lengths of silk trailing down her back.

"Chisha is coming around?" she asked Thea hopefully, her black eyes glowing.

"Yup! She even had dinner with us and didn't make a single snarky remark! I think we've had a breakthrough!" Thea was still a little wary of the older woman, but she was willing to give the new attitude a shot. Daeshen was thrilled with the change in his mother, and Thea wasn't going to do anything that might make Chisha start behaving badly again. It was hard sometimes; Thea was still feeling defensive around her. She had to force herself to not take everything Chisha said as an attack. The woman had the tact of a charging bull.

"That's good news!" Sya'tia seemed pleased. "Come down to the kitchen. Corvin wanted to talk to me about something and you guys need some dinner. He said you didn't stop for lunch." She shook her head and made a tsking noise. "Sandwiches on the road! You need a good meal, my loves!"

They trooped into the kitchen like good little soldiers while Sya'tia continued to scold them for not taking better care of themselves. Several minutes later, they were seated at a round table in the kitchen while Kokia placed dish after savory dish in front of them and urged them to eat.

Sya'tia told them quietly her mother had been cooking all day. Kokia had wanted to show off her culinary skills when Sya'tia had told her how much Thea enjoyed cooking. Apparently, Sya'tia's mother had great plans of stealing Thea away later to trade recipes.

Sya'tia's family would be joining them tomorrow morning for breakfast. There was still too much work in the fields for them to come to the house for dinner. Kokia mentioned that a school of nibblers had invaded the fields and the family and hands were going to have to stay in there all night to keep them from eating the new crops.

"What's a nibbler?" Thea asked as she sampled a piece of fish in some kind of yellow sauce. The flavors exploded in her mouth. She moaned with pleasure. "Oh my, this is wonderful!" She eagerly forked up another bite while Kokia beamed and answered her question.

"That's just a nickname. They are actually called *dorya*, and they love new sea ferns. They can eat an entire crop in a night. Usually, they aren't a problem here, but the weather has been so warm that they are moving more. It's a large group too. It's too bad we don't have any resident meechas. They love feasting on nibblers." Kokia spooned more food onto Corvin's plate. "You are too skinny! Eat, eat!"

He laughed and continued to pack away the food. It was one of Thea's favorite things about him. He loved his food. She wondered why he wasn't married. Corvin would be a wonderful father and needed someone to take care of him. He was frequently so involved in his work that he forgot to eat. Thea had started checking in on him to make sure he did. She often took him plates of food around dinnertime because he was usually still in his office and completely oblivious to the time.

They demolished the food on their plates, but it barely made a dent in the amount Kokia had made. When they were all full, they leaned back in their chairs and sighed happily. The whole meal had been wonderful!

Corvin looked at Sya'tia with a wary expression. The food was all put away and they had settled down to enjoy an after dinner cup of tea. Thea got an uneasy feeling.

Corvin tapped his finger against the side of his cup with a thoughtful expression. Thea felt her stomach knot. This didn't look like it was going to be good news.

Corvin shook his head and looked up to meet their eyes. "Sya'tia, I would like you to give me the care of your eggs from now on instead of allowing them to be stored with the general populace."

Sya'tia's black eyes narrowed and fixed on his face. "Why?" she asked, her face becoming expressionless.

Corvin squirmed uncomfortably. "Um, because I asked?" he ventured, looking hopeful.

Daeshen snickered.

Sya'tia's lips twitched. "Not good enough, my friend."

He didn't move for a moment, then he took a small box out of his bag and set it in the center of the table. "I found that the Council had scheduled your eggs for destruction to prevent the possibility of..." he seemed to struggle for words, "hereditary birth defects."

Sya'tia flinched as if struck.

Thea reached for her hand and held tight.

"I see," the Warrior Chosen said in a tight voice. Her hair curled in on itself and braided into a tight protective knot at the back of her neck. It was the only sign of how the words had hurt her.

"There is *nothing* wrong with my daughter!" Kokia broke in. Her expression took on a fierce cast as she defended her daughter.

"Of course there isn't, Kokia. She's amazing," Thea said soothingly.

Kokia leaned back in her chair, looking satisfied with this agreement. She smiled fondly at Sya'tia.

"I took your eggs," Corvin continued, his gaze locked on Sya'tia's face. Thea knew he didn't want to cause Sya'tia any pain, but it had to be said. He wasn't the kind of man to let her keep going through the motions of letting her eggs be harvested when they would only be destroyed.

Daeshen frowned thoughtfully. Thea could almost see the wheels turning in his brain.

"Won't you get in trouble for taking the eggs when they were supposed to be destroyed?" Sya'tia asked him quietly.

Corvin squirmed. "Maybe, but I don't care. Until you sign the release they are, legally, still your property."

Daeshen smiled evilly. "They are? We didn't know that." He cackled softly. "Sya, why don't you call your sisters and cousins tomorrow? If they are your eggs, you can give them to anyone you want, and since your family members share your genetics, the Council can't argue an increased risk of birth defects." He looked very pleased with himself.

Corvin looked at Daeshen with an arrested expression. "You are absolutely right! And the Council cannot deny an entire family the right to reproduce." His eyes gleamed. He turned to Sya'tia's mother. "Lady Kokia, I would not impose, but we have more than a full month planet-side. Would you permit me to stay as long as possible to allow the ladies to reach the right cycle for implantation if they wish to have a child?"

Kokia smiled. "You are welcome for as long as you wish to stay, Doctor. On behalf of my family, I would like to thank you for the service you have done my family and my daughter. You are truly a man of substance."

Corvin's cheeks turned pink. "Thank you," he murmured, looking embarrassed. He stuffed the box back in his bag.

Kyrin patted the table. "Well, that's settled nicely. How about a swim to work off some of the delicious dinner? Kokia, we'll all have to roll out of here after a month of your good food!"

Kokia flushed and hummed with pleasure.

Thea really liked Sya'tia's mom and couldn't wait to meet her sisters. Kokia seemed thrilled to have them visiting and Thea was looking forward to getting to know her better. She smiled wryly to herself. Two out of three great mothers-in-law weren't bad odds. And if Chisha didn't get any friendlier, Thea could always slip her a key lime pie, which acted like an aphrodisiac on the Ta'e'sha. *Bet she'd be really interesting then*, Thea thought to herself with a smidgen of cruel delight.

She slid a sideways look at Sya'tia. She sent a tendril of feeling toward her and was pleased when Sya'tia grasped it and sent back a pulse of love. She didn't seem too upset by the conversation; in fact, she seemed pleased. Thea would talk to her about it later. Right now a swim sounded great.

Chapter Seventeen

Thea floated aimlessly through the roomful of women. Sya'tia's cousins and sisters had descended upon the house like a swarm of locusts the day after she had called them. Fifteen women, all wanting babies. Sya'tia had twelve eggs, so they were trying to decide how to parcel them out. It was actually a good time for them to become pregnant. The timing would allow the babies to be born in early winter, the quiet time for the family's farm.

She hadn't realized how many people lived in the cove! There were twenty families down there! It boggled her mind, but now she understood why there was a parking lot built off to one side of the house. She had thought it was for the farmhands who lived in town.

She paused to reply to a greeting from one of the women. They were all extremely friendly and had many questions about humans. Everyone seemed very excited about Sya'tia's engagement and wanted to throw a party to celebrate. Thea had been hauled into a corner to talk about when the party should take place. Several of the women were asking her to create tapestries for their homes also.

They all wanted silk.

She wasn't sure how it would hold up to long-term water emersion, though, so she told them she would look into the matter. Another woman had asked if she had tried some of the Ta'e'shian yarns and threads yet. That had sparked a long conversation about textiles, which she had thoroughly enjoyed.

Sya'tia's family reminded her of some of the ranchers and farmers she remembered from her childhood. They had the same love of the land and waters that made up their home.

Her family was very different from both Kyrin's and Daeshen's. Both of the men came from affluent families that were involved in more cerebral occupations. Kyrin's family seemed to focus on financial analysis and consulting and Daeshen's family had been in politics for several generations.

Sya'tia had two mothers and three fathers. Thea had realized early on that Sya'tia didn't see a distinction between the man and woman who had given her life and the rest of her parents.

That is why Daeshen had been so angry with his mother. By rights, Chisha should not have cared who had fathered Thea's child since both husbands were considered fathers. By claiming it was Kyrin's child, she had excluded Daeshen's rights to their child. It was a subtle way of saying Daeshen was not truly married to Thea or Kyrin.

Sya'tia's male relatives had immediately dragged her husbands off to do guy stuff. She wondered if that involved stag flicks and beer. They were very excited about getting to know both Kyrin and Daeshen. She had learned Sya'tia's family was bursting with pride over Sya'tia's accomplishments. She was the first Chosen born in their family for the last five generations. But they had been worried that no one would look past her "birth defects" to see the woman underneath.

Sya'tia hadn't had an easy life and the whole family was fiercely protective of her. Kokia had confided that they had been thinking about setting Sya'tia up on blind dates so she could meet some eligible men.

Thea would have loved to videotape that. The poor men would have run screaming the first time Sya whipped out one of her knives for them to admire.

The arrival of more people dragged her attention back to the present.

"Thea!" a voice screeched.

Thea blinked in surprise as she was swept into a bone-crushing hug. "Cristabel?" she asked, wheezing.

The redheaded Amazon released her and grinned. "We've missed you! Sya called and asked if we'd like to come up for a visit."

Zinnia hugged her next. "How have you been?" she asked in her quiet, reserved manner.

Thea smiled and kissed them both on the cheek. "Great! I've missed you guys! Is Ruri here too?"

"She's here; I think she was saying hi to Sya. Wow, this place is awesome! Shage is with his family. They are really nice, and man, did his mom rip a strip off him when she found out what he did!" Cristabel bounced on the balls of her feet with enthusiasm. "She rocks!"

Zinnia smiled fondly at her wife. "His family is wonderful. Cris and I have been talking, and we *might* have his babies. At least, I will. The thought of sleeping with a guy still gives Cris the heebie-jeebies." She ran a hand down the taller woman's back. "It turns out he has a very nice lady friend he wanted to introduce us to. He's got a crush on her. We'll see."

Sya'tia came charging over to pick Cristabel up and give her a huge hug. "My war sister! Greetings and welcome to my home!" She beamed and pressed kisses on both of Cristabel's cheeks before setting her down again. Next, she turned to give Zinnia a much gentler hug. "Hello, lovely one. My heart sings that you have come."

Zinnia blushed with pleasure. "It's good to see you as well, Sya. Thank you for your invitation."

Sya'tia had fallen in love with both women as soon as Thea had formally introduced them. She and Cristabel had found that they had several things in common. They had started working out together. Apparently, sweating was a great bonding experience for both women. Thea smiled inwardly as she watched them chatter animatedly. It was a little surprising though, since their occupations were completely different. Sya'tia was a pure warrior and Cristabel was a physical therapist. Zinnia, she had later learned, was an accountant. She thought that occupation perfectly suited the quiet woman's personality.

Ruri slinked over and gave Thea a quick hug. "How ya been, babe? I hear you got a nightmare mother-in-law," she said in English as she slung an arm around Thea's shoulders.

Thea curled an arm around Ruri's waist and hugged her lightly. "Chisha? She's coming around. It's hard to outstubborn me. Besides, Daeshen pretty much told her off before we left her house. She actually apologized to me and, from Daeshen's reaction, hell must have frozen over because of it," Thea replied in English.

Ruri and Sya'tia had forged a tentative friendship in the months since the fight had occurred. Thea was very pleased with the effort her friend was making. She was even getting along with Kyrin and Daeshen. Ruri had finally talked to Kiger a bit about how she felt. Thea had gone with her to have the conversation. Kiger was appalled by how his behavior had been hurting his wife and had immediately tried to make amends. Since that day, Ruri had been calming down and was actually learning to like her husband. Thea had high hopes like would turn to love. Kiger was a pretty great guy, and just as clueless about women as her young friend Soren. Soren still stuttered and tripped whenever he spoke to a member of the opposite sex. Well, except Thea and Sya'tia. He was very relaxed around both of them.

Kokia came up to them. She was wearing another of the kimono-style robes she seemed to favor. This one was decorated in seashells and anemones. "Hello! You must be Thea's sisters! I'm so happy you could come! Welcome to our family!" She kissed each of the women in greeting.

Thea quickly made introductions. There was a brief flurry of confusion over Cristabel and Zinnia's short hair, but Thea managed to explain to Kokia that human women had more leeway for hair length and that it did not mean that Shage had stolen children.

Kokia dragged them off to be fed, and after that, show them to rooms. Thea was glad that the house was so big!

Corvin came to her. "Wow, what a group. Did I just see some of the ladies from the ship?"

Thea nodded. "Sya'tia invited them to visit."

"Excellent," was his contented reply.

Thea turned to eye her friend. "How are the exams going?"

"Very well. As soon as we know who's getting eggs I can get started monitoring them for fertility cycles." Corvin looked very pleased with himself as he continued to watch the swarm of women laughing and chatting together.

"Have they figured out a way to decide?" she asked curiously.

"I don't know," he replied with a smile. "Sya'tia suggested a knife throwing contest but I believe that was vetoed." He moved off to answer a question from one of the women.

Thea grinned and wandered into the kitchen where her friends were eating. "Hey, guys, how's the food?"

Cristabel winked and continued chewing.

Zinnia carefully wiped her mouth with a napkin before answering. "Excellent for all that I have no idea what I'm eating."

Thea poured herself a cup of tea and sat down with them. "I've found it's best not to ask."

Ruri looked up from her plate. "Kokia reminds me of my grandmother."

Thea smiled, but didn't reply. There was something subtly different about her friend. It was as if the rage had been blunted.

"What have you guys been up to?" she asked instead.

They told her about the things they had seen and done since landing. The warmth in the room, the camaraderie, was soothing. For all that Thea loved spending time with her new families she had missed her friends.

After a while the conversation wound down as each woman finished telling her about her experiences. "Let's meet tonight, out by the water. I want to tell you about the trial. The Lord and Lady made several appearances."

The women sucked in startled breaths and started shooting questions at her.

"*Live?*"

"They're here?"

"What are They like?"

"Are you serious?"

"Oh my freaking God!" this from Ruri.

"Exactly," Thea murmured.

Before they could say more, Sya'tia's father, Velian, barged into the room. He was a huge bear of a man with white hair and blue skin a few shades darker than his daughter's. He reminded Thea of Triton from Disney's version of *The Little Mermaid*. He had broad shoulders, washboard abs, and a wide grin. In a word: hot. "I hear I have new nieces! I want hugs and names!" He threw open his arms and beamed at the women expectantly.

The witches stared at him, bemused.

Cristabel bravely threw herself into the breach and hugged him. "I'm Cristabel, this is Zinnia, and this is Ruri," she said, introducing the other women.

Velian grinned broadly and waved his hands at them. "Hugs!" he demanded in a deep voice.

They got up to hug him as ordered.

Satisfied, he flopped down at the table next to Thea. "Ahhh, such exotic beauties! Welcome to the family!" His eyes gleamed at he studied each of them appreciatively. "Tell me about yourselves!" He leaned back in his chair, folded his arms across his chest, and gave every sign of being willing to stay there all day if that's what it took.

Cristabel was the first to start, and the other women soon began to join in the conversation. Thea smiled inwardly. Before he was done, Velian would pull every detail he wanted out of them and they wouldn't realize it till later. He was so easy to talk to you just didn't think about it.

She was very happy to be part of this family. Life was good.

Later that night she kissed her husbands and fiancée as they prepared for bed. "I'll be back later; I need to talk to the girls privately, okay?"

Kyrin frowned and nodded. "Take a jacket; it's getting cool." He stole another kiss. "We're gonna start without you," he added with a leer.

She giggled and skipped out the door.

Ruri was just shutting the door to her room. Thea traipsed over and bowed dramatically. "Madam Wench, shall we adjourn to the night?" she whispered in sepulchral tones.

Ruri laughed softly and they crept down the hallway like they had hunchbacks.

Cristabel and Zinnia came out of their room and stared. Without a word, Cristabel assumed the position and lurched after them, growling nonsense in a dramatic accent.

Zinnia sighed, shut the door gently and followed them.

Someone had to be the adult and Thea was just glad it wasn't her tonight. She giggled and leered comically back at

Zinnia who laughed and shooed them down the hall. She had so much to tell them! Thea hoped they were just as happy about what she had to say!

Chapter Eighteen

Thea sighed contentedly as she dropped several bags onto the floor of her family's cabin. It was good to be home.

Daeshen, Kyrin, and Sya'tia came in behind her. They also dropped several bags and boxes. Sya'tia's family had sent them away with many gifts and lots of love.

As much as she had enjoyed her time planet-side, she was glad to return to the ship. It had become her home and she had missed it.

A sound made her turn. Her husbands froze beside her.

A huge jaguar stood in the doorway. His fur was smooth, clean, and shining with health. He yawned majestically before sitting on his haunches. His mouth dropped open slightly in a feline grin. "*You're home. I have missed you, mind-mate.*"

Thea swallowed. "I know you. You were in my dream."

Kyrin sucked in a wheezing breath behind her. Sya'tia came to stand beside her, watching the cat warily. Daeshen didn't move a muscle.

"*Of course. The Lady let me meet you before I decided to come,*" was his blasé reply. He looked at Kyrin. "*We'll be good, Captain. Our assignment is finished.*"

Kyrin grumbled under his breath at that.

"*My name is Condezl and I would be proud to be your familiar, Theadora. Will you accept me?*" His golden green gaze fixed on Thea intently.

Thea smiled slowly. "I would be proud to call you my companion, Condezl, and thank you for the honor of choosing me."

"*Excellent!*" Condezl chuffed softly with satisfaction. "*Now, can we talk about raw silk cat beds? I'm thinking teal...*"

Thea laughed; this was going to be fun. "Of course! Shall we adjourn to my workroom, kind sir?"

Daeshen stared after his wife as she walked calmly beside the huge cat. "What's next? A wolf?" he asked no one in particular.

"You barfed in my shoe!" Kyrin suddenly bellowed at the cat.

Mental laughter floated through everyone's mind as the door to Thea's workroom closed gently.

Epilogue

Gaia landed on her ass. She looked around irritably. More points of color appeared around her. Skye and the Ta'e'shian Lithen popped into existence and also landed on their best-padded parts one by one.

She stood up and rubbed her abused seat. "What's going on?" she asked.

Kashka flicked her tail and propelled herself upright in a fluid motion. "I don't know."

The Great One appeared with a theatrical shower of multicolored sparks. "I wanted to talk to My children," boomed a sexless voice filled with pleasure. "I have been watching your shenanigans and I am pleased with the way you worked together during the trial. It was truly an example of give and take. I am proud of you. And now I have another task for you."

They gathered around the Great One and listened.

"You will go to Earth and prepare my lands," the Great One said at length. "The Ta'e'sha will need what I have hidden. They will need it soon."

"Which lands need to be prepared?" Gaia asked.

The Great One began to fade from view. "Atlantis."

~ * ~

Glossary of Terms

Arkaa -- planet where samples are to be collected

Arkaana -- ace of humanoid spider people

Asana -- Priest(s) and Priestess(es) of the Lithen; group term

Byasuen -- Goddess of Craft and Arts (Ta'e)

Cerebcom -- technology implanted in the brain to allow communication between a ship's artificial intelligence and/or another individual who also has an implant

Chosen -- individual of Ta'e'shian society who is born with markings showing they are favored by the Gods

Com -- to send a communication to someone using an implanted cerebcom

Corgan -- motorized object used to pull someone through water at high speed

Creamstal -- powdered shell of a sea snail, used in cooking

Crystalshroom -- type of mushroom that secretes a liquid that hardens upon contact with air, used in artwork

Chrystarea -- sea flower, blooms once every seven years

Deema -- affectionate term for "father"

Dorya -- small fish that travel in large school, also known as nibblers

Ecoha -- God of Craft and Arts (Ta'e)

Felbos -- messy sea creature; similar to a monkey

Gaia -- generic name used to refer to Lady of Witches (Goddess)

God-marks -- features used to identify Chosen of the Gods

Holoreader -- a small flat computer used in place of paper

Iliria -- Goddess of Healing (Ta'e)

Kashka -- Goddess of Warriors (Ta'e)

Kyen -- Gentleman, or gentlemen

Kysout -- God of Soul Renewal (Ta'e)

Lavoya -- dinner dish made with seafood, dish title, not an ingredient

Lith -- single set of Gods and Goddesses of the Ta'e'sha

Lithen -- Gods and Goddesses of the Ta'e'sha as a whole group

Meecha -- animal native to Ta'e

Mo'aton -- God of Healing (Ta'e)

Samonan -- Goddess of Soul Renewal (Ta'e)

Saras -- shape shift; to change one's form

Sea Fern -- food plant, grown and used similarly to wheat

Sha'ki -- moon of Shya, to be terraformed

Shaysha -- Goddess of Spiritual Balance and Mental Healing (Ta'e)

Sho'bi -- moon of Shya, to be terraformed

Shoomoe -- dinner dish of fish fillets and fried vegetables

Shya -- planet to be terraformed

Skye -- generic name used to refer to Lord of Witches (God)

Solune -- God of Spiritual Balance and Mental Healing (Ta'e)

Sparker -- wire suit, used as a sex toy

Tabet -- Goddess of Atlantis

Teirnan -- God of Atlantis

Vosh -- God of Warriors (Ta'e)

 THE END

Theolyn Boese

Theolyn Boese lives in Oregon with her wide assortment of animals, which include two cats, Goblyn and Stupid (yes that really is his name and well earned), a Border Collie named Fuzzbutt, a few ducks, and her pheasant, Samurai.

She has been writing since grade school, staring with a poetry class her teacher enrolled her in to help her learn to work with dyslexia. Bolstered by her teacher's faith in her she quickly learned to love reading and writing instead of being afraid of it. Soon after she was reading voraciously and scribbling poems on everything.

She would love to hear from her readers and invites them to write to her at Sabrielle@gmail.com, and to check out her website at http://www.theolynboese.com.

TITLES AVAILABLE In Print from Loose Id®

DAUGHTERS OF TERRA
THE TA'E'SHA CHRONICLES, BOOK ONE
Theolyn Boese

FORGOTTEN SONG
Ally Blue

LEASHED: MORE THAN A BARGAIN
Jet Mykles

THE ASSIGNMENT
Evangeline Anderson

VETERANS 1: THROUGH THE FIRE
Rachel Bo and Liz Andrews

VETERANS 2: NOTHING TO LOSE
Mechele Armstrong and Bobby Michaels

Publisher's Note: The print titles listed above were previously released in e-book format by Loose Id®.

Non-Fiction by *ANGELA KNIGHT*
PASSIONATE INK: A GUIDE TO WRITING EROTIC ROMANCE

LaVergne, TN USA
13 November 2009
164057LV00002B/8/P